MW01643763

Nick

A SHADOW OPS TEAM NOVEL

Makenna Jameison

This book is a work of fiction. Names, characters, places, and incidents are the product of the author's imagination. Any resemblance to actual events, locales, or persons, living or dead, is coincidental.

Copyright © 2024 by Makenna Jameison

All rights reserved, including the right of reproduction in whole or in part in any form.

ISBN: 9798320897011

ALSO BY MAKENNA JAMEISON

ALPHA SEALS CORONADO

SEAL's Desire
SEAL's Embrace
SEAL's Honor
SEAL's Revenge
SEAL's Promise
SEAL's Redemption
SEAL's Command

Table of Contents

Chapter 1

Nick Dowd swiped his badge and strode into Shadow Security Headquarters, nodding at the receptionist. Clara was on a call, and he continued across the vast lobby, his sneakers squeaking on the shiny floor. He headed for the doors leading to the basement, which housed the armory, gun range, and large gym. He'd gone for a run on his lunch break but wanted to put in some time on the weights as well. Nick felt keyed up and on edge, and he hustled down the stairs, pulling open the door to the state-of-the-art facility. His mind had wandered as he'd lapped the grounds of headquarters, the cold winter air doing little to clear his torrent of thoughts. He grabbed a water bottle, taking a long chug, and unable to resist, pulled his cell phone from his pocket. Nick frowned as he reread the messages from a month ago, lines of worry etched across his forehead.

Kaylee's text was uncharacteristic of her, not to

mention completely out of the blue. Although he'd kept in touch with his ex despite all the years that had passed, it was more 'how's your family?' and 'hope you're doing well.' Christmas and birthday type stuff. Seeing her name when a message popped up always sent a jolt of awareness coursing through him, filling him with a warmth he couldn't entirely explain. It might've been a damn lifetime ago that they were together, but his body always responded to hers on a primal level. Kaylee had a hold on him in a way he'd never fully understand, despite the miles between them and years that had gone by.

Once again, he looked over the month-old texts. Nick had been about to board a plane to Egypt with his teammates when he'd unexpectedly gotten a message from Kaylee.

Kaylee: I need your help.

Nick: Are you okay? I'm getting ready to catch a flight, but tell me what's going on.

Kaylee: Call me when you're back. It's important.

Nick: Tell me what's wrong.

Nick: Kaylee.

Kaylee: I need to hire you.

Nick: What?

Kaylee: I need a bodyguard.

Nick's stomach had roiled at the implications of that. What danger could Kaylee possibly be in? She was a freaking graphic designer in Nebraska. He didn't know exactly where she was working these days, but it's not like she was running black ops missions like him. Was an old boyfriend giving her trouble? Was it something else?

Kaylee was currently single, as far as he knew. That didn't mean she couldn't have had a date gone bad, a stalker…. His mind had already been running through possible scenarios.

Nick hadn't even seen her in over a year. He'd been home visiting his parents, and they'd run into one another. Seeing her at the bar that one night was like a bolt of lightning, brightening the area and electrifying the room.

Kaylee had still been gorgeous as hell—silky dark hair with those pretty green eyes. A petite body that fit perfectly against his. And her curves. Hell. Nick's teenage self hadn't been able to get enough of her. He still remembered exactly what she felt like beneath him, her body soft everywhere he was hard, her trusting gaze locking with his own as he'd made love to her. He'd never felt more alive than when he'd been with Kaylee. Years had passed, and they'd both dated other people. Taken separate paths in life. Moved on.

His gut clenched at the idea of another man's hands on Kaylee. He couldn't stomach even thinking about it, but Nick had no claim on her, no right to her body or heart.

Not anymore.

The out of the blue text from her had been startling. She never would've asked for his help if she didn't truly think she was in danger. Kaylee was level-headed and smart. Nick had wanted to call her right then and there and demand to know what was going on. He'd sent Kaylee one last text before hopping on the flight to Cairo. While he might not be active-duty Army anymore, the Shadow Ops Team that he was part of deployed all over the world. Kaylee had no clue that he was still going on missions, taking jobs that Uncle Sam couldn't or wouldn't do. As far as she knew, Nick worked for Shadow Security, guarding clients.

The truth was far more complicated and not something he'd ever burden Kaylee with. They'd broken up all those years ago for a reason, needing to take their separate paths in life.

Nick shook his head, frustrated. Kaylee had always been too good for him. Innocent and trusting. Wicked smart. He was a crack shot with his weapon, but sitting behind a computer screen would never be the type of life he wanted to lead. Nick needed a physical job, to be in on the action. He went where the military had sent him, his duty to God and his country. His career was even more dangerous now, without the protection of the government at his back.

But Kaylee? She was supposed to be safe at home, following her dreams. What the hell had she gotten involved with that required his protection?

"What are you thinking so hard about?" Sam Jackson asked, startling Nick out of his thoughts. Sam crossed the gym at Shadow Security Headquarters to where Nick stood.

Nick's gaze flicked over his friend and teammate, taking in his workout gear. He hadn't even heard the large, muscular man come in, which was saying something. Nick was always on alert. Only thoughts of Kaylee could make him lose his edge like that. "Eh. It's nothing."

"It's the girl," Sam said with a smirk.

Nick raised his eyebrows.

"Before we went to Cairo, you were texting someone. A woman. You even called her your old flame," Sam recalled, his gaze all too knowing.

"Of course you'd remember that," Nick muttered.

"Yeah, well, you've been distracted ever since we got back. You even missed a shot at target practice the other day. That never happens. Besides, Gray's the guy on the team who's usually all brooding and shit. Something's bothering you."

"I'm surprised you noticed," Nick quipped. "Hasn't Ava been keeping you busy?"

"God damn, she has," Sam said with a wicked grin. "She's safe in my bed, exactly where she belongs. Thank fuck we saved her in Cairo," he said, looking serious for a moment. Their recent op had unfolded quickly, with Ava unknowingly being hired by a terrorist intent to harm the U.S. The sculptures she'd been commissioned to make were a means to an end, meant to be smuggled onto U.S. soil with chemical weapons inside. The team had swooped in to save her, thwarting the plot, with Sam and Ava getting back together after they'd returned from Cairo.

"I'm glad she's okay," Nick said. "That was a hell of an ordeal for her to go through."

"Same. That doesn't mean I haven't noticed something is going on with you, man."

Nick lifted a shoulder. "It's complicated. Kaylee and I were together when we were young, but that was a lifetime ago."

"So why the hell was this girl texting you before Egypt?" Sam asked, his brows narrowing. "How'd she even get your number?"

"We've kept in touch over the years," Nick admitted. "If ever there was a case of the timing being bad, this was it. We were both too young back then. I wasn't ready to settle down. Besides, I couldn't drag her into the Army life, always waiting and wondering if I was okay. We broke up. Moved on."

Sam crossed his arms. "Last I checked, we're civilians now."

Nick rolled his eyes. "Yeah, all safe and sound here in upstate New York. Bullshit. If anything, the work we do is even more dangerous now."

"She didn't like that you were enlisting back then?" Sam questioned.

"She was proud of me, but we both had some growing up to do. She graduated high school and went off to college. Got a job. She's had boyfriends over the years but nothing too serious, as far as I know. Clearly, I'm still single."

Sam snorted.

"Honestly, I figured she'd have settled down by now—gotten married, had a few kids. Maybe that didn't fit into my lifestyle or career choice, but Kaylee? She's incredible—"

Sam was smiling, a shit-eating grin on his face.

Nick shook his head. "Never mind. The point is, we text each other around Christmas and birthdays. That's it. Right before Cairo, completely out of the blue, she shoots me a text and says she needs my help."

"With what?" Sam asked, the smile disappearing off his face.

"She wanted to hire me as her bodyguard."

"Shit."

"Yeah. I told her I was about to get on a plane but would call her when I was back. It just about killed me to not know what was wrong, but what could I do? This is my job. We're always deploying on ops."

"Cairo was a while ago," Sam said dryly.

"It was. When I did reach out to Kaylee after we were back in the States, she sent me a vague text saying not to worry. I did, of course, because wanting to hire me was a strange request. She never explained what that was about, just blew it off. But then my birthday was last week—"

"And you didn't hear from her."

"Nope," Nick said. "I want to think it doesn't mean anything, but I can't shake the idea that something's wrong. Kaylee was finishing high school when I enlisted in the Army, but I always heard from her on my birthday. She'd text me when she was in college, afterwards. Even when she was dating some schmuck, she'd still shoot me a text just to say happy birthday. This doesn't add up."

Nick scrubbed a hand over his jaw. When he'd returned from Cairo a month ago, she'd practically ghosted him, only saying not to worry, she'd be in touch when she could. Like he wouldn't worry about the one woman he'd ever truly cared about. That was like asking the sun not to rise one day. She'd been a part of him ever since he was young and dumb, forgoing a future with her and instead heading where the Army sent him. He sure the hell wasn't ready to marry her when he was eighteen, and then life had moved on. If a part of him regretted letting her go, so be it. Nick knew all too well that life didn't always turn out like you planned.

"You think she's in trouble," Sam said.

"Why the hell else would she need a damn bodyguard? That's out of left field."

"What's out of left field?" Shadow Ops Team leader Jett Hutchinson asked as he strode into the gym, dressed in a polo shirt and pressed khakis, a stack of papers in one hand. He had about ten years on the rest of the team but was still incredibly fit, sharp, and lethal. He moved quietly toward them, not unlike the way a panther might stalk his prey. Jett was always alert, even in the building he owned, at the company he'd built. His gaze focused on the men as he assessed them.

Nick's eyes met those of his boss. "Just a girl."

Jett's lips quirked. "Ah yes, the fairer sex. Not that my Anna would enjoy being called 'fair.' Fierce is more like it," he joked, referring to his new bride.

"You can say that again, boss," Sam quipped.

Nick crossed his arms, listening to them banter for a moment. Jett had been their team leader back in their Army days. When they'd all left the service after a mission gone bad, Jett had formed Shadow Security and recruited the others to work for him. Most of the public thought they were in the security business, providing bodyguards and security detail to clients. They did some of that to maintain their cover, but the Shadow Ops Team ran black ops for the government, taking on missions the Feds couldn't. Jett took jobs from his government contacts, sending in the team when they were needed. It was risky, dangerous, and adrenaline-fueled work, and Nick wouldn't change his career for the world.

"Yeah, well, this girl is more level-headed than fierce," Nick said. Kaylee couldn't have been more different from Jett's wife. Kaylee was beautiful but always calm and in control. Focused. Anna was a firecracker, all wrapped up in a sexy little package. She wasn't Nick's type at all, even before she'd become his boss's wife. Anna and Jett balanced each other out, despite their differing personalities. A woman like Anna would drive Nick batty.

Jett leveled him with a look. "Is this the same girl

from last month?" he questioned.

Nick stiffened. Clearly, he wasn't as secretive as he thought if even Jett had noticed his concern. "Just worried she's in trouble, boss."

"Where does she live?" Jett asked.

"Nebraska."

Jett nodded as if he'd known that all along. "Go check up on her. You're from Omaha, right? Head home for a couple of days and figure out what the problem is. I need my sniper to have his head in the game, and you deserve some down time. You've been going on nonstop missions for months. The guys with women all took some time around the holidays. You need some R&R as well."

Nick let out a breath. "I didn't need—"

"That's an order," Jett said. "If your girl is in trouble, you'll hate yourself for sitting on it when you're trained for all types of shit hitting the fan."

"She's not my girl," Nick countered, shaking his head. "We dated when we were young. It's been years—a lifetime ago."

"All the same, it's been on your mind. Take care of this—of her," he stressed. "You're concerned, and I can appreciate that. You've got good instincts, so I believe that you have reason to worry. If there's a problem, notify the team so we can handle it."

Nick raised his eyebrows.

"Don't look so surprised. We take care of our own," Jett said, his eyes hardening. His gaze shifted toward Sam before landing on Nick again. "We're briefing in thirty about the Mexico op. I don't anticipate us needing to move in for a week or more. After the briefing? Catch a flight to Nebraska. I don't want to see you in the office tomorrow." He waited until Nick nodded and then turned and walked back out of the gym without another word.

Nick's gaze lifted to his buddy's.

"Guess that's that," Sam quipped.

"Guess so," Nick said, a new feeling winding through him. He was anxious to find Kaylee and learn what was going on. Nick wouldn't feel settled until he made sure she was okay. If his body still took note anytime she was near, well, so what? He was a grown man. He could table the feelings he'd always seemed to harbor for her. Ignore the heat and adrenaline coursing through him.

After he checked up on Kaylee, Nick could go back to his regular life. Work. Gym. Missions. His gaze flicked over to the weights, and he felt more focused than he had in weeks. "I've got twenty minutes to lift, then I need to grab a shower before the briefing. After that, I'm looking up flights to Omaha."

"Damn straight," Sam agreed. "Go get your girl."

Chapter 2

Kaylee Thomas muttered under her breath, sliding her burner phone into her pocket as she wove her way through the parking lot. Leaving the safehouse the Feds had put her in weeks ago might have been stupid, but she couldn't sit still any longer, waiting to learn what was happening, wondering if they really had her best interests in mind. Something had felt off about the entire situation from the moment they'd whisked her away. It's not like she'd been placed in the Witness Protection Program. Kaylee had temporarily been shuttled somewhere safe, away from her family and friends. Certainly, police or Federal Agents could have guarded her small apartment if they really felt she was in danger. Instead, she'd simply vanished. They'd taken her away from her old life and kept Kaylee in a constant state of waiting.

She pulled her hoodie more tightly around herself as she shuddered.

Kaylee watched as a mother pushing a shopping cart full of groceries passed her, two crying toddlers keeping her hands full. The woman's life looked so ordinary, mundane even, if not for the cranky kids. She was grocery shopping for crying out loud, no doubt clearly on her way home.

Kaylee's gaze tracked across the parking lot. The bus ticket she'd purchased earlier that morning had taken her hundreds of miles away from her own home. The Feds said they'd told her parents that she was somewhere safe the night they'd whisked her to the safehouse, but had they? Kaylee was starting to doubt that they were actual Federal Agents.

She gripped her backpack more tightly, mentally cataloging the contents. Clothes. A few toiletries. Laptop. Granola bars. Cash. She had her wallet, but if she actually used any of her credit cards, they'd locate her.

Was she running from the people she worked with or from those supposedly tasked to keep her safe? It didn't matter at this point. She was far from home and needed to keep it that way. Maybe she should've gone straight to the authorities and told someone what was going on.

Ten minutes later, she was heading out of the grocery store, a jar of peanut butter, box of crackers, two bottles of water, and some apples in her plastic grocery bag. Kaylee had no idea what to do and couldn't afford to spend a lot on food until she figured it out. Plus, she didn't want to cart it with her if she had to flee again. She'd get a cheap hotel for the night and figure out a plan.

The wind whipped through her, and she shivered. Too bad her coat and boots had been in the front area of the safehouse. She'd left with barely more than the clothes on her back, slipping through the window in the hours before dawn and fleeing.

"Are you okay?" a woman asked.

Kaylee blinked, realizing she'd frozen in place, then pasted on a smile. "Yeah, fine. Just daydreaming. I better get going," she said, lifting up the single plastic grocery bag she was carrying. Kaylee hurried on her way before the woman questioned her further or she drew too much attention to herself. This was a small town, and certainly, people would remember a stranger. At least the bus had dropped her in the business section. There was a motel down the street, and it would have to do for the night.

Kaylee started walking on the sidewalk, taking in the shops and stores. It looked like a decent enough place to stay for a few days. Come to think of it, however, she should continue on her way tomorrow. The more distance she put between her and her hometown, the better. Until she knew who those people really were, she couldn't risk them finding her. She'd taken exactly one bus to get here. If anyone starting searching the cities and towns the buses went to directly from Omaha, she'd be relatively easy to find.

A few minutes later, Kaylee handed over some cash to the woman at the front desk of the motel. Thankfully, they'd had some vacancies. It didn't look like there were any other options within walking distance. This place was old but seemed safe enough, at least for a night. It's not like the parking lot had been full of drug dealers or prostitutes.

"Are you in college, hun?" the woman asked.

Kaylee had always been on the petite side, but it

was probably more the backpack and hoodie that gave her the college student look right now. "Yeah. I'm just visiting for the night."

The woman nodded like she'd expected exactly that, handing over a key to a motel room. "Check out is at ten. There's no restaurant here at the motel, but I always recommend the diner down the street."

"Great. Thanks."

Kaylee took the key, the cool metal biting into her hand, and then moved to the elevator. No one else was around at the moment, but it was late afternoon. She assumed later this evening guests would be returning from whatever had brought them to this sleepy little college town. And while she'd love a hot meal at the diner, that wasn't going to happen either. She needed to stretch her cash for as long as she could.

Dumping her backpack onto the faded bedspread once inside the room, Kaylee fired up her laptop. While she'd been made to leave her cell phone at her apartment when they'd whisked her away last month, they'd allowed her to bring the laptop. At least the motel had Wi-Fi. Kaylee opened the browser, searching the news for Omaha. There was nothing about her disappearance, no mention of her name or a missing woman, so maybe the people who'd hidden her away really had notified her family. She worried her lip. No one was looking for her.

No one except the people she'd run from.

Kaylee let out a frustrated sigh. She was never in the office on Sunday evenings, except that once, and then—she shook her head, trying to push away her memories. It was little use, because they played like a movie reel in her mind.

***

Kaylee swiped her badge and moved into one of the secure areas in her office building, passing through the quiet, empty cubicles. Staff were on duty elsewhere, but she wasn't in the branch of her division that required coverage twenty-four seven. The graphics Kaylee designed went into other classified reports—not current, pressing intelligence that might be required in the middle of the night. Too bad she'd accidentally left her wallet in her desk. She'd managed without it all weekend but needed to go grocery shopping. At least she'd had her work badge to get into the building.

Voices suddenly drew her attention. Only the higher-ups had an actual office with a door, although this one was clearly wide open. The offices lined the perimeter of the space, and she slowed, sensing something was wrong.

"Just let me take a peek," a woman's voice said, and Kaylee heard the low murmur of a man. "You have it with you, right? Show me."

Kaylee stilled. She didn't hear the man's response.

"Your wife doesn't know I'm here," the female voice continued. "She just thinks you're working late. Let me take care of you first."

Kaylee heard the sound of a zipper, and then a male groaned. "Fuck. Let me see your tits, baby. That feels so good."

"You like?" the woman asked teasingly, and then Kaylee heard the distinctive sounds of clothes rustling and a couple having sex right there in the office. Grunts and moans filled the silent space, and she felt nausea rising within her.

"Shit," Kaylee muttered, quickly turning away. She accidently knocked a tape dispenser off of a cubicle desk in her haste, the sound thumping on the ground of the otherwise quiet vault.

"Someone's here," the man said.

Kaylee bent to retrieve the tape, and as she stood, a military officer was already coming out of the office, adjusting his clothes. Kaylee might be a civilian, but she worked closely with her government and military counterparts at Offutt Air Force Base. While she didn't know his name or rank, she recognized him.

His sharp gaze landed on her.

"I forgot my wallet," she said quietly, feeling nervous. "I'll just quick grab it from my cube."

The military officer narrowed his eyes and watched her as she hurried away. That wasn't his office anyway. Had he and the mystery woman just grabbed a dark room to have sex in? Her heart pounding, she yanked open her desk drawer and grabbed her wallet, fumbling with it as she slid it into her bag. Kaylee took a deep breath, hoping they were already gone.

When she walked back around the corner, the mystery woman was sliding a phone into her purse. "Thanks for the fun, baby," she purred. "And the photos."

"Quiet down," the man chastised, still inside the office.

Kaylee's jaw dropped as she realized the woman was someone in HR. Although she had a low-level clearance, she shouldn't have access to any intelligence reports. And she damn sure shouldn't have a cell phone or camera in a secure area of the building. The woman didn't see Kaylee and quickly walked in the other direction, her hips swinging in her tight skirt.

Kaylee froze in place. Should she go to security? Contact her boss?

The man stormed out of the dark office, papers in his hand, and stared at Kaylee with an icy glare. "I need a word with you." He began to move toward her, his face hard.

She turned and ran.

***

Kaylee blinked, and her gaze focused again on the tiny motel room. The bedspread that she was currently sitting on had clearly seen better days, and she tried not to cringe as she imagined how many people had slept there before. There was a small TV, dresser, and an old but clean bathroom. She'd bolted the door but would probably shove the chair in front of it later to feel safer.

Kaylee closed her eyes for a moment. Would she ever feel safe again?

She'd learned the military officer's name was Colonel Mike Cornwell. He'd been having an affair with a woman in the office, funneling classified intelligence to her. Kaylee had been whisked away that very evening by men saying they were Federal Agents, allegedly to protect her as a witness. But Kaylee hadn't been fully interviewed by anyone. She hadn't been able to contact her own office. Kaylee had been taken from her apartment that night, only allowed to gather a few things, and then—poof! They'd whisked her away. She'd shot off a couple of texts when she'd been quickly packing, before leaving her phone behind as she'd been instructed.

Briefly, an image of Nick, her ex-boyfriend from years ago flashed though her mind. She'd texted him asking for his help. Nick had been leaving, however, readying to catch a flight. He was a busy man, even outside of life in the Army. The company he worked for was known to be the best of the best. Shadow Security provided bodyguards and protection for their clients—protection she needed.

Had he tried to call her? Had he forgotten all about it?

She shouldn't have agreed to leave her phone at

her apartment. What if someone else had accessed it, contacting her family and friends? What if everyone thought she was okay?

Kaylee bit her lip, feeling chilled to the bone despite the fact that she was inside her motel room. She should text Nick again. If he knew she was in trouble, he'd help her.

Kaylee picked up her burner phone.

Chapter 3

Nick walked across the tarmac of Offutt Air Force Base in Omaha, the cold wind biting into him. He braced against the weather, his duffle bag slung over his shoulder, his jacket zipped up tight. Jett had called in a favor, getting Nick on a military flight to Nebraska. It wasn't conventional in the least, but it turned out Jett had a buddy that owed him a favor. He had contacts all over the world, an advantage that had served him well in forming Shadow Security. Nick could've easily ridden commercial, but given the timing, this had worked out better than he could've hoped. His gut had been telling him something was wrong, and now that he'd landed in his home state, he wished he'd come here sooner and found out why Kaylee had asked for help.

Nick's credentials allowed him access on base, and he moved freely toward one of the buildings. He might not carry a military ID anymore, but Shadow

Security had clearances to enter a multitude of government facilities and military installations. There were more than eight thousand military and civilian personnel employed by Offutt, but he was thankful he didn't need an escort to move around. He'd already waited too damn long to come and was anxious to find out answers.

Kaylee hadn't responded to his text earlier asking if she was okay. He'd even called her, and it had gone straight to voicemail. Nick didn't even know her address aside from the fact that she still lived in Omaha. Her parents still lived in her childhood home. He'd go pound on their door if he had to. It wasn't like her to blow him off, especially after she'd asked for his help. Something was wrong.

"Dowd!" a male voice shouted, and Nick's head swiveled to the left as a man in fatigues moved toward him. Life in the military meant multiple TDYs, PCSs, and deployments. Nick knew service members stationed around the globe. That didn't mean he expected to run into any of them the moment he landed at Offutt.

A smile broke out across his face as he saw Everett "Ace" Walker, the leader of the Alpha SEALs Coronado team. Nick didn't know Ace too well but had met him on a joint op years ago during his Army days. Ace's commanding officer was Jett's brother, Commander Slate "Striker" Hutchinson. While Jett had left the military behind, Slate still very much remained faithful to his career in the Navy and led multiple SEAL teams on the West Coast.

Nick grinned at his old buddy. "What are you doing here, man? This isn't exactly sunny Southern California."

"Negative. I was here on TDY. And no, I didn't join the Air Force," Ace joked.

"I figured as much. So, what's the deal? They needed some Navy guys to do their job? We all know Army is better," Nick razzed.

Ace chuckled. "My CO asked me to brief some of the brass on base about a recent op. It's a bit unusual given I'm not a briefer or analyst. They wanted intelligence from the boots on the ground, so to speak, so here I am. Normally, a secure video conference would work, but I happened to be flying cross country and made the stopover. We just finished up a little while ago. What are you doing here?"

"I came home to check up on some stuff, and Jett got me a ride other than commercial," Nick explained.

"Oh yeah? Sounds like Jett—always the rulebreaker."

Nick smirked. "Damn straight. He called in a favor from a friend. I saw your CO at Jett and Anna's wedding not too long ago."

Ace chuckled. "Yeah. Our commander couldn't believe it when Jett first started dating her, but I guess it worked out. The CO said his brother seemed happy as hell."

Nick shook his head, trying not to smile. "He is. And man, Jett and his brother couldn't be more different."

"A fact he's mentioned more than once," Ace said with a grin. "So, you're from Nebraska?" he asked, glancing toward a plane that was loading in the distance. Nick followed his gaze, realizing Ace was readying to go wheel's up.

"Guilty as charged. I'm from Omaha."

"Your family's here," Ace assessed.

"They are, but this doesn't involve them. I just need to check on an old…friend."

Ace shot him a knowing look. "Gotcha. Well, I hope it works out for you, buddy."

"Thanks, man. I'll let you go. Looks like your ride is about ready," he said, nodding toward the plane Ace was heading to.

"Yep. I gotta get back to Coronado. There're several things on the horizon—as always, right? Tell me, do you miss the Army?"

Nick chuckled. "Not at all. We're still running ops, however, as you know. It's been good for our team. These are the same men I served with."

"They're damn good guys," Ace said.

Nick clapped him on the back. "That they are. Have a good flight, man."

"Thanks. Good luck with your situation," he added. The men briefly shook hands, and then Ace was heading off to hop his flight back to the West Coast. Nick shook his head. When he was still in the Army, Nick and his teammates had been Delta Force. They'd handled counterterrorism, hostage rescue, and reconnaissance missions. Life on the Shadow Ops Team was similar, only without the government to back them up. If anything happened to any of them on foreign soil, they were on their own.

Nick continued toward the building, ready to catch a ride. He needed to stay focused on his goal here—find Kaylee, make sure she was okay, then get back to his real life. His gut churned with the idea that something was wrong.

Grabbing his phone once again, he shot her

another text.

Nick: I'm in Omaha. Let's meet up. Call me.

There was no response, not that he was surprised. It would be too much to hope that she'd suddenly reply now that he was here in Nebraska. Frowning, he shoved his phone back into his pocket. It felt like there were about a million things on his mind, but he'd start with the easiest—going straight to her parents.

***

"What do you mean you haven't heard from her?" Nick asked an hour later, frowning as he stared at an older version of Kaylee on her parents' front porch.

Karen Thomas worried her lip, exactly in the same manner Kaylee always did. Karen once had dark hair like her daughter, but it was now salt and pepper gray. She was petite, with similar facial features to Kaylee. Staring at her was like looking into his future—seeing what Kaylee would look like in thirty years. The thought was a little jarring. What made him picture growing old with his ex-girlfriend? Memories washed over him, mixing with his concern.

"Exactly that, Nick. Kaylee told us something was going on about a month ago and said that she might have to leave for a little while. She didn't explain much at all, just said that it was urgent. A couple of days later, a man came to visit our home to let us know she was okay. He looked like an FBI Agent, although he never showed us his badge."

Alarm bells went off in Nick's head, and he scrubbed a hand over his jaw. Clearing his throat, he eyed Kaylee's mom. "What did he tell you?"

"He said that she was safe, and he'd be in touch when he could tell us more."

Nick frowned, not liking the sound of any of it. "Mrs. Thomas, is it okay if I come in? I'd like to ask you a few questions."

"Of course," she said, looking flustered. "I'm sorry I didn't invite you in right away. I was shocked to see you here at my front door, although I know you and Kaylee have kept in touch over the years. I'm somewhat relieved you're concerned as well. My husband said not to worry, but something feels wrong."

"It does," he agreed as he stepped through the front door. His eyes drifted to the stairs as Karen closed the door, turning the lock. Although Nick and Kaylee had dated as teenagers, he'd only been up to her childhood bedroom a handful of times. They'd snuck around anyway though, getting lost in each other in his own bed while his parents had been at work or making love in the back of his truck. He'd never been able to get enough of her, and thankfully, the feeling had been mutual. She'd been nervous but eager for him, and when their bodies moved in sync, joined together as one?

Shit.

He didn't need to be remembering any of that now. Years had passed, and they'd both moved on.

His gaze scanned over the pictures in the hallway, drinking in the photographs of her. His heart pounded in his chest as he took in her fair skin and gorgeous green eyes. One fairly recent photo was of Kaylee on a beach, her sundress clinging to her curves. Both affection and lust coursed through him. She might've been beautiful as a teenager, but hell.

Kaylee was an absolute knockout now.

And he'd let her get away.

"Did you just arrive in Omaha?" Karen asked, eyeing Nick's duffle bag as he set it in her foyer.

"Yes, ma'am. I caught a flight to Offutt," he explained. "My former commanding officer was able to get me on board a plane."

"Wow. That worked out nicely. You're working for a security company now, right? I understand you left the Army."

"Yes. I'm with Shadow Security. We provide protection and act as bodyguards for our clients," he said, relaying to her what was on Shadow Security's public website.

"That's wonderful."

"Thank you."

"Have a seat," she said, directing him toward the sofa. Nick's phone buzzed in his pocket as he crossed the living room, and he pulled it free, frowning as he realized it was from Gray. Of course, it wasn't Kaylee. For all he knew, she'd never even seen his recent messages.

Gray: Let me know if you need any help.

Nick: Will do.

Gray: I'm serious. Say the word and I'm there.

Nick: Got it. Thanks, man.

"Just my buddy," he explained as he took a seat. While he hadn't chatted with Gray about his concerns regarding Kaylee this afternoon, Jett had told Nick after the meeting that he'd arranged for a flight. No doubt Sam had filled in the rest of the team after he left. It felt good to know his teammates had his back. The problem was, he had no idea what sort of trouble Kaylee could be in. Nick was starting from square one, gathering intel about his former love. While he'd love to rush right in and solve the problem, he was currently sitting in the dark.

Half an hour later, his mind was whirling. Kaylee wasn't doing marketing with her graphic design skills as he'd imagined. She was a civilian contractor for the DEA. She made graphics for highly classified reports—materials her parents had never even seen. Kaylee had never mentioned where she was working during their text exchanges. In fact, he knew little about her life now despite the fact that they'd kept in touch. Uneasiness wound through him. Was her disappearance tied to her work? What else hadn't she told him?

He let out a breath. "I assume you've been to her apartment?" Nick asked. "I don't even know her address but figured I could get it from you."

"No, we actually haven't been there recently. The FBI agent who came to our home assured us that Kaylee was safe but asked that we stay away from there. He didn't want us to draw any attention to ourselves," Karen said, looking worried. "My understanding was that they were protecting her as a witness to something. He didn't disclose any details as to what or provide additional information."

"Did he actually say he was FBI? The Witness Protection Program is run by the U.S. Marshal Service, not the Bureau."

"I don't think he specifically said what agency he was with. The man identified himself as being with the government. Gosh. I was so worried; I don't even recall every detail. I wish we had one of those doorbell cameras that recorded everything. I did try to call her that night, but her phone rang and rang. I wondered if I should go to the police, but this man said the government was protecting her. I just don't know what to do."

Nick watched her intently. He didn't want to alarm Kaylee's mom, but in his experience, the Feds were usually eager to flash a badge. This wasn't someone undercover gathering intelligence, who wouldn't want to disclose where he worked. A supposed Federal Agent showing up on Karen's doorstep but not providing her with his credentials was suspicious.

"Do you have any contact info for the agent you met?" Nick asked. "A name or cell number for this guy?"

She shook her head. "He assured us he'd be in touch again soon. I was so upset, I didn't even think to ask him for it."

"But you haven't heard from him since then."

"No, just that once," she said, wringing her hands together. "That was weeks ago, Nick. I felt like we should trust him. Kaylee had said she might need to leave for a little while, so of course I figured it was related. I just expected to hear from her long before now."

"I had no idea that she was a contractor for DEA," Nick said, letting out a breath. "If she works there, she has clearances and access to all types of classified information."

Karen looked sympathetic. "She didn't want you to worry about her."

Nick stared at her in disbelief before shaking his head. "We kept in touch but aren't exactly close anymore. When we broke up, we made a clean break."

"You were both so young when you were together.

She's dated over the years, of course, but she never settled down, never started a family. I think a part of her has always loved you," Karen said, her voice sad.

Nick stilled.

Kaylee was happy. Wasn't she?

"We barely know each other anymore," he finally said, his voice catching. Karen didn't respond, and Nick felt uneasiness stirring within his gut. He'd moved on. He'd dated over the years, had casual girlfriends. Hadn't looked back. Just because Kaylee stood out amongst all his exes didn't mean they were meant to be together. Nick was a realist. It hadn't worked out, and that was that. He was lying to himself, however, because he knew damn well that no other woman would've reached out to him like this and known he'd come.

"I'm here because she asked me for help," he said as he stood up from the sofa. "Can you give me her address? I'd like to check things out. After that, I'll reach out to her employer. You mentioned she's on a DEA contract, but do you know the name of the company she works for? I'd appreciate it if you could write that down along with any other contact info you have for Kaylee. All I've got is her cell number, which she's not answering."

"Of course. I'll get all that for you before you go. I'm so worried," Karen admitted.

Nick reluctantly met her gaze again, wishing he could say something to reassure her. "Me too."

Chapter 4

Kaylee clutched the burner phone in her hands, listening to the other end of the line ring. She'd tried Nick earlier, but his number had gone straight to voicemail. For all she knew, his phone was turned off because Nick had been on a flight again. He could be on the other side of the world right now, unable to help her. She could contact Shadow Security directly, but she didn't know anyone else there. Kaylee couldn't exactly use her credit card to pay for their services—not without someone potentially finding out her location. She'd run for a reason, and Kaylee instinctively knew that the men who'd hidden her away would be looking for her.

"Please pick up," she whispered as Nick's phone rang again.

She looked around the sparse motel room, feeling lonely and scared. The heater beneath the motel window was barely keeping up with the winter weather, and she shivered at the chill in the air. Kaylee had been running on adrenaline since sneaking out of the safehouse, but now that she'd finally stopped? She was trembling, both cold and frightened. Tears smarted her eyes. What was she supposed to do? Kaylee was about to end the call when suddenly Nick's gruff voice answered.

"Hello?"

A different kind of shiver raced down her spine at hearing his voice.

She hadn't spoken to Nick in more than a year, when they'd run into one another in Omaha. He'd looked good then—more muscular than when they'd been teenagers, but still tall and lean, with a gruffness and alertness about him that came from years of military service. Nick was the total package—smart, strong, lethal. He was a full-grown man now, not the teenage boy she'd once fallen in love with. She'd watched him that night, noting the differences. Nick was harder. Intense. His broad shoulders, corded forearms, and veined hands had been intriguing when he'd approached her. But she hadn't missed the way his eyes had grown hot as they looked her over.

Every time she'd seen him over the years, her body still went on high alert. Her cheeks flushed. Her heart rate increased. He'd once known every inch of her body, kissed and caressed every part of her.

She'd had boyfriends over the years, but no one serious. No one who made her feel the way that Nick did. They'd merely chatted for a bit that night, dancing around the obvious attraction they still felt for one another, and then gone their separate ways. He'd been meeting some old friends, and he'd left her to her own evening. Their groups had briefly mingled at one point, Nick shooting her the occasional look, but that was it.

Seeing a man she felt nothing for shouldn't have been that hard.

And that was the kicker.

Kaylee feared she'd never truly gotten over her first love.

"Hello?" Nick asked again, and adrenaline spiked through her veins.

She cleared her throat, finally finding her voice. "Nick? It's me. Kaylee," she added, hating that she had to even mention that.

A beat passed. "Kaylee?" he asked in surprise.

"Yeah. I'm sorry to call you out of the blue like this, but—"

"I'm at your apartment," he said abruptly, shocking the hell out of her.

"You're in Omaha?" Kaylee was dumbfounded. She'd texted him a month ago asking for help but never expected him to fly out there and literally show up on her doorstep, especially not after all the time that had passed since then.

"I just came from your parents' house. Your mom gave me your address, even though we both knew you wouldn't be here. I wanted to come check things out for myself. Where are you? Are you okay?"

"Yes. No. I don't know," she said, flustered. "You saw my mom?" she asked, her heart racing. "They told me they'd contact my parents to let them know I was okay, but I didn't know what or who to believe. Is she okay?"

"She's okay but worried about you. Who told you that they'd speak with your parents?" he asked, and Kaylee could hear the concern in his voice. "Hang on.

I probably shouldn't talk right in front of your apartment. Just give me a sec. I'm heading back to my rental car."

She heard movement, a shuffling sound as Nick jogged down the stairs, and then a car door slammed a few seconds later. "Okay, I'm inside my vehicle. I haven't checked it for bugs but just picked it up today. We should be able to speak freely."

Bugs. Not the creepy crawly kind. She heard him starting the engine. "Wait, why'd you go to my apartment if you knew I wouldn't be there?"

"I wanted to look around, see what I could find. Your mom gave me your spare key. I was just about to go inside when you called me. And I can't tell you how relieved I am to hear your voice," he said, and Kaylee could hear the truth behind his words. "No one knows where you are. I was hoping to find a clue or something so I'd know where to start."

"That's just—wow. Okay. I still can't believe you flew to Omaha to check on me."

"And I can't believe you're calling me right now," he countered. "What number are you calling from anyway? This isn't your cell."

"A burner phone. I just bought it today. I'm scared, Nick."

She heard him swear in the background. "Where are you? Your mom explained the basics, but I'd like to hear from you exactly what's going on, and I'd prefer we talk in person. I'll come to you, and then you can fill me in on everything."

"I'm not in Omaha."

The line was quiet for a moment, then Nick cleared his throat. "Are you still in Nebraska? Or should I head to the airport?"

Kaylee blinked in surprise. "You'd jump on another airplane and come to me."

"Of course I would. You might've said you needed my help and then blown me off afterwards, but—"

"What do you mean I blew you off?" she asked, confusion coursing through her.

"I texted you after I got back, and you said not to worry. Then you never responded to my texts or messages after that," Nick said, his voice gruff.

"Nick, I left that same night. I texted you and said that I needed a bodyguard, but then I was whisked away by the men who showed up at my door. That wasn't me who sent you the message about everything being okay."

"Damn it," he swore. "I knew something was off when I didn't hear from you on my birthday. I've been worried," he said.

Kaylee let out a breath. "I'm sorry. I thought I was safe where I was being held, that I was being rushed away from my regular life for my own protection. I would've tried to contact you sooner if I thought I was in immediate danger. They put me in a safehouse and told me not to have contact with anyone. After a week or so, I was beginning to doubt everything. No one would fill me in, and I still couldn't contact my family. I had no idea what was really going on. I finally snuck out and took a bus out of town. I'm several hours away from Omaha and not even sure if I should stay here more than one night."

"I'll come get you," he assured her. "I've got a rental car. You can explain everything once I arrive, and we'll figure this out together. If it's something big, well, I've still got my contacts from the Army. You won't have to deal with this alone."

"Okay," she said, her voice breaking. She swiped away the tears, thankful he couldn't see her, and sniffled. The last thing she needed to do right now was fall apart.

"Hell. Don't cry, Kaylee," he said, his voice husky. His words washed over her, soothing her in a way she hadn't even realized she'd needed. Nick was former military. A bodyguard. He could protect her physically, but until that moment, she hadn't realized he could still protect her emotionally as well.

"I'm okay," she said, her voice trembling. Kaylee shivered again in the motel room, wishing he was already there.

"I'm going to help you," Nick assured her. "Text me your address, and I'll get there as soon as I can."

"I'll send it when we hang up."

"Okay. We'll figure this out, I swear. I promise that I'll keep you safe," Nick vowed.

"Thank you," she whispered, emotions swirling within her. She and Nick hadn't been a couple in well over a decade. He had no reason to go out of his way for her right now, but she couldn't deny there was still a connection between them. She'd felt it a year ago at that bar, and she felt it now, despite the miles separating them.

They said goodbye and ended the call, and then she was fumbling with her burner phone, texting him the address of her motel. It would be several hours before he arrived. She was on-edge but knew she'd feel calmer once Nick got here. It was in his nature to be protective, solving problems and watching out for others.

And until he arrived late that night?

She'd do her best to stay calm and hope like hell that he would know what to do to help her.

Chapter 5

Nick pulled onto the interstate, his eyes moving again to the rearview mirror. Someone had been following him since he left Kaylee's apartment complex, and he needed to lose the tail, stat. He glanced up again after he'd merged onto the highway, trying to memorize the plate. It was backwards in the reflection, but he could make it out in the waning light. He recited the letters and numbers to himself, committing them to memory, then sped up. He'd call his team to run a trace once he lost the car following him.

He switched lanes, moving around a truck, and cursed when the vehicle on his tail made the same maneuver. They weren't even trying to be evasive. Or maybe they thought he was clueless, not realizing he'd been followed. Whoever was tailing him had no idea who Nick was or what he was capable of.

Nick stayed in his lane, speeding up as they approached an exit. At the last second, he pulled off, watching as the other car sailed past him, slamming on their brakes.

Nick checked his mirrors as he took the exit, the other car disappearing as Nick took the curve of the ramp. The GPS on his phone automatically rerouted him. He could pick up the interstate again in a few miles. Pushing a button, he called Gray. His other teammates would be happy to jump in, but they all had women now. Some of them had kids. He didn't want to bother them right now unless it was urgent.

"What's up?" Gray asked, his voice low on the other end of the line. Nick heard the crack of the cue ball in the background, and then a muffled sound as Gray headed somewhere quieter.

"I need you to run a plate for me—get with West. I need it tonight."

"Will do. Did you find out anything about your girl?"

"She's not my—never mind. Yeah, I heard from her. She's gone into hiding but called when I was about to search her apartment earlier."

"You work fast," Gray said with a low chuckle.

"I got the keys from her mom," Nick said. "Kaylee and I go way back. It was dumb luck that she called me when I was outside her door, but I'm not complaining. She's not in Omaha, so I'm going to her. I don't know what's going on or who she's hiding from, but someone was tailing me when I left her apartment complex. You ready for the tag?"

"Yep. Give it to me."

Nick recited the license plate. "I lost them, but her place is being watched. Kaylee was in protective custody—or being hidden by someone impersonating a Federal Agent."

"What the fuck?" Gray asked. "Where is she now?"

"A motel several hours west of Omaha. I'm heading to her now. I don't know why she's hiding, but I'm damn sure about to find out. I'll probably have to move from her current location, because I doubt any motel she found is secure, but at least she'll be with me."

"Let me know what else I can do. I'll get back to you on the plate tonight."

"Thanks. I appreciate it."

"Watch your six," Gray told him.

"Always do." Nick ended the call, his gaze continuously scanning the area. It was getting darker out, which would make it harder for anyone to follow him. He'd gone a couple miles and was about to take the ramp onto the highway again. Hopefully the mofos on his tail were long gone, but Nick knew they'd be looking for him. For her. Kaylee was still several hours away, and he felt restless, the urgency of the situation sending his pulse pounding. Something was very wrong if her place was being watched, and he wouldn't feel better until he laid eyes on her, ensuring for himself that she was safe.

***

Three hours later, Nick was pulling into the outskirts of the little college town. He could see lights from bars and restaurants several blocks down, but the motel was in a quieter area. He scrubbed a hand over his jaw, waiting for the traffic light to change. He'd been running on adrenaline since he landed hours ago and was tired yet anxious to see Kaylee.

The drive felt like it had taken forever, the distance between them shortening as the minutes ticked by.

The light changed, and a minute later, he turned into the parking lot. Nick pulled into a space, glancing at his phone as he momentarily left the engine running. Nothing. Gray had texted earlier, saying they were working on finding out who owned the vehicle tailing Nick. He thumbed a quick message to Kaylee, and she responded with her room number. Moments later, he was striding toward the motel, duffle bag slung over his shoulder.

He hadn't totally thought this through, because he hadn't been planning to bunk with Kaylee tonight. They might've spent plenty of time together in bed long ago, but that was in the past. If she was truly in danger, however, he wasn't about to leave her alone in an unsecured motel room.

Hell.

Nick jogged up the stairs to the second level, his gaze sweeping the area as he moved in the dark. His sidearm was tucked into his waistband, but he was lethal even without a gun. Nick was a highly trained operative, and it would take someone with a skill to get the jump on him right now.

A door opened as he moved closer, and then Kaylee's head peeked outside. His heart thundered at the sight of her, but he cursed, wishing she'd stayed inside the room. If anyone had followed Kaylee or Nick to the motel, she'd just given away her precise location.

"Kaylee," he said, his voice gruff. Her look of fear had briefly disappeared at the sight of him, but just as quickly, her distress was back, and she glanced toward the dark parking lot. "Let's go inside," he urged, his voice gruff even to his own ears. His hand landed on her arm without thought, and then he was guiding her in, his big body blocking her own in case anyone was watching them from down below.

Nick's gaze swept the small space as he turned to lock and bolt the door. There was a small double bed and armchair, neither of which looked too comfortable. He'd sleep on the floor if he had to tonight in order to keep her safe.

"You brought your stuff," she said unnecessarily as he slung his bag to the ground. He didn't miss the way her gaze traveled over his muscled forearms. Nick kept in good shape and didn't hate Kaylee's eyes on him. Not in the least.

She flushed as she realized he'd caught her staring, but Nick decided to ignore her reaction to him for now. "Are you okay?" he asked, his voice lower than usual.

The moment between them felt private—intimate. They were locked inside a motel room together, and his first priority was to make sure Kaylee was truly all right. His gaze tracked over her, drinking her in. She wore a hooded sweatshirt over a white tank top, and he tried not to stare at the way it stretched across her breasts. Her jeans clung to her like a second skin, and her face was flushed, her lips parted. She looked good. Damn good. He tried to ignore the hint of cleavage and the way her denim jeans hugged her ass and thighs. Nick's body had immediately taken notice, however, and he felt his dick twitch. Kaylee was a knockout, all flushed and beautiful, standing mere feet in front of him.

She was also in danger. Scared.

"I'm fine," she said, but the wavering of her voice

betrayed her.

Nick kept a respectful distance from Kaylee—as much as he could in the tiny motel room, at any rate. His hands itched to touch her, to ease the fear written across her face. She'd always fit perfectly in his arms—and felt like she'd been made for him alone when she was stretched out beneath him, their bodies moving together as one.

"I brought my bag up because I didn't want to leave anything in the rental. I was followed when I left your apartment earlier," he said.

"You were followed?" she asked in surprise.

Nick hated seeing the worry in her eyes. Unable to stop himself, he finally stepped closer, brushing back a strand of her silky dark hair. He might have no right to touch her, but it was hard to stay away. He'd once known her entire body intimately. He wanted to explore all of the woman she'd become, but the need to soothe and protect her took precedence above all else.

"A car followed me after we spoke earlier. They tailed me on the highway once I left your apartment complex. Someone was watching your place."

Tears welled in her eyes. "Shit. Kaylee." He drew her in for a hug, feeling her body meld against his own, her vanilla scent filling his nostrils. Her arms tightened around him, and he could feel her trembling. Nick slid a hand down her back reassuringly, needing to keep her close. "It's okay. I lost the tail. No one knows that I'm here. We're safe for tonight, but you'll have to tell me what's going on. We can keep moving in the morning, maybe even go back to New York."

"To Shadow Security?" she asked as she pulled back.

He lifted a shoulder. "It's a more secure location. It might be good to disappear for a while, and I can keep you safe there. We can figure out what exactly is going on. I work with a lot of my old buddies," he said, licking his lips. Energy was already coursing between them, despite the nature of their conversation. His body had always reacted to hers on a primal level.

Her green eyes tracked over his face, lingering just a beat too long on his mouth. "God, Nick. I just can't believe any of this is happening."

She stepped back, but he took her hand, loving the feel of her smooth skin against his own. She looked so damn fragile and delicate beside him. He'd always been a lot bigger than her, and he'd loved that. Now it just made him realize how much more vulnerable that made her. Kaylee was his to protect, even if she didn't know it yet. A part of him had always belonged to her, and he'd do whatever was necessary to keep her safe.

Kaylee clung to his hand, pulling him over to the bed. The gesture wasn't sexual in the least. She needed someone to hold on to, and Nick was happy to be there for her. She sat down on the edge of it, clutching onto him as she began telling him what she'd witnessed.

"You think they were stealing classified information," he said once she'd finished explaining what she'd seen a month ago.

"I know they were. No one should've had a camera or phone in the secure area."

He scrubbed a hand over his jaw, his other hand

sandwiched between Kaylee's. He wasn't sure she even realized she was still clinging onto him, but he loved that after all these years, she still trusted him to keep her safe.

"I didn't even know you were on a DEA contract," Nick said. "I thought you were in marketing."

She shrugged, looking slightly embarrassed. "I was but got a new job a year or so ago. We didn't really tell each other a lot about our lives, Nick."

He looked down at their joined hands, clearing his throat. Even though Kaylee was scared, he couldn't deny how fucking right it felt to have her close, clutching onto him. Her vanilla scent and smooth skin were tempting as hell. He wasn't about to lay her down on the bed and do all the things he was dreaming of, but he'd be lying if he said being near Kaylee didn't affect him. "You're right. We didn't share a lot of details after we broke up. I'm not sure I'd have wanted to hear about any boyfriends of yours over the years."

Kaylee gripped his hand more tightly. "You dated, too, Nick. You left Omaha behind and went off to see the world. I know you weren't single all this time."

"I wasn't," he said, his voice thick with regret. "We agreed breaking up was for the best."

"Was it?" she asked, and his head swiveled toward hers in surprise. "Never mind," she muttered. Kaylee let go of his hand and stood, pacing the room. Nick wanted to know why she'd said that, but it was hardly the most pressing matter right now. Kaylee was in danger. He'd have to sort out his feelings toward her later—either that, or bury them back where they'd been for the past decade. She still lived in Omaha, and Nick was still deploying on missions all over the world.

"I don't know who those guys were that shuttled me to a safehouse that night," she said. "They acted like they were FBI, but now I'm not so sure. I never saw a badge. I didn't tell anyone what had happened yet, either. I rushed back to my apartment in surprise. I'd gone into my office because I accidentally left my wallet there and needed to go grocery shopping. The next thing I knew, two guys in suits were at my front door."

Nick shifted on the bed, frowning. "What's the standard protocol for your office when something like that happens?"

"We'd report it to the Security Information Officer. I was planning to go in early Monday morning to speak with him. There's a regular security desk in my building and of course guards at the entrances to base. I should've told someone," she said, sounding frustrated. "I could've gone straight to my supervisor at DEA or even my own employer. I figured not saying anything until the next morning would be all right."

"You did what you thought was best," Nick assured her.

"I knew something was off," she said, shaking her head. "They knew who I was and showed up at my apartment within the hour. If I hadn't reported it yet, that meant someone else at Offutt or within DEA knew what was going on. They acted like I was a key witness to an ongoing investigation and leaving for a little while would be for my own safety."

"Whoever was involved got access to your personal information. If you were in a secure space,

I'm assuming you had to badge in. Someone there accessed that."

"Yeah," she said, worrying her lip. Kaylee was still pacing, playing with the zipper on her hoodie. The material fell to the side, revealing a creamy shoulder. Her breasts were rising and falling, pushing against the white tank top as her breathing sped up. Nick stilled. He had no right to want her, but God damn, he did.

Pushing those thoughts aside, he focused on the back of her head as she turned and strode the other way, still agitated. "What's the name of the military officer you caught sharing classified information?" he asked.

She whipped around, her gaze landing on him. "Colonel Mike Cornwell. I only found that out afterward, because I don't directly work with him. We didn't know each other before that night."

"And the woman?"

"She's in HR. I forgot her name but could find out. I don't think she would've known exactly who I am either. I only recognized her from HR training. She wouldn't know me from my face alone."

Nick nodded. "One of them had access to the security databases or knew someone who did. They found out who badged in at that time, got your name, and then went to your home. If the men who you believed were FBI or other Federal Agents came to your apartment immediately after what you witnessed, someone at Offutt or DEA sent them."

"They wanted me out of the way, so I couldn't report them. But what happened to that classified intelligence? She was photographing some materials Colonel Cornwell had."

Nick's fist clenched. "The materials could've been sold already, unless they were waiting for the right buyer. Either way, you witnessed what happened, and that puts you in jeopardy. They already identified you."

Kaylee let out a breath. "So, what should I do? I feel like I don't even know who to trust right now. I don't know if anyone else was involved." Her chest rose and fell again, and he could see the fear in her eyes.

"We need to find the extent of who's involved in this. I'll have my team work on it."

"Your team of bodyguards?" she asked skeptically.

"There's stuff about me you don't know either."

She looked at him, her green eyes wide, and the vulnerability he saw there slayed him. Nick clenched his jaw as he stood, slowly moving toward Kaylee. If he was going to help her, she deserved to know the truth. "Shadow Security does provide bodyguards to clients, mostly former government officials. I do other work, too. Go on missions."

Kaylee let out a breath. "You never got out of the Army?"

"I'm out of the Army. I run missions on a black ops team now."

Chapter 6

Kaylee pulled slightly back, staring at him in shock. Nick was looming in front of her, his entire body tense and alert. She could see his chest rising and falling, the material of his shirt stretching across his pecs. He might have a runner's build, but he was solid muscle. Nothing but pure male strength. He'd been a sniper in the Army, from what she recalled. The man was lethal—both his looks and skills. She could see it now—the patience, the restrained strength. He might've left the military, but it was still every bit a part of him.

"You're on a black ops team?" she echoed.

Kaylee knew he was a bodyguard but figured it was more of a formality, escorting former government officials around safely. He worked for a security company. He guarded clients.

How wrong she had been.

Nick moved closer, and she felt the heat from his

large body, his slightly musky scent filling the air between them. It wasn't cologne, just whatever soap he used and pure Nick.

Raw. Masculine. Virile.

"Kaylee," he said, reaching out.

"Don't," she snapped, tears smarting her eyes. "I was worried about you every day that you were deployed, and I thought you were safe now. I thought you were okay." The tears began spilling over, and then he was collecting her in his arms.

"Shhh," he murmured, his hand smoothing over her hair.

She felt his hard body pressed against hers and soaked in his strength and warmth, awareness coursing through her. He'd been here mere minutes, and she was already falling apart. Kaylee whimpered against Nick, trembling as he held her. He was still putting his life in danger after all these years, and now Kaylee was in danger, too. Nothing she knew made sense anymore, and as Nick tightened his arms, awareness of his firm muscles and raw masculinity washed over her, complicating everything.

"It's okay," he assured her. "We'll both be okay. My Army training got me to where I am today. Our missions are fully sanctioned by the government. My former commanding officer recruited us to join his company when we got out of the military. Jett runs the Shadow Ops Team himself. We take jobs the Feds can't or won't do."

"But you—you're supposed to be out of all that," she said, pulling back as she tearfully looked at him.

He raised an eyebrow.

"I want you to be safe," she said, her voice faltering.

Nick's large hand rose to cup her cheek, his thumb smoothing over her skin. Even now he was trying to soothe and comfort her. His other hand landed on her hip, squeezing gently. He was holding her to him, she realized, keeping her from pulling away. Her eyes searched his as the air between them grew thick, her admission hanging there. Maybe she wasn't supposed to still feel anything for him, but this was Nick. She'd always care about him.

"I hate that you were worried about me," he said, his voice gruff. "But I would do anything—anything—to keep you safe."

The air between them grew thicker, and she felt the same pull she always did when he was near.

Nick moved in, seemingly without thought, his lips landing on hers. Her hands spread across his hard pecs, and she could feel his thundering heartbeat. He wasn't as unaffected as he appeared. His hands moved then, one sliding to the back of her head, tangling in her hair, the other pressing against her lower back, drawing her closer. He held her the way he wanted as he took her mouth, deepening the kiss, their bodies pressed together.

Kaylee gasped and opened to him, letting Nick take complete control. His tongue slid into her mouth, and she felt her panties growing damp, her nipples pebbling. His touch always sent her up in flames, and she both loved and hated that he still affected her this way years later. His erection pressed against her stomach, and she felt a throbbing in her sex. She still wanted him. Badly.

"Kaylee," he breathed, drawing back as they both gasped for air. "Tell me to stop." Nick's eyes were wide with arousal, his body tense, and she could tell he was hanging on by a thread. He'd stop if she asked him to, but then she'd always regret not getting one more night with him.

Kaylee gripped his biceps, searching his gaze. "And if I don't want you to stop?"

"I didn't come here tonight to make love to you," Nick said softly. "I can hold you. Keep you safe."

"I want you," she whispered urgently.

No other words were needed as he backed her towards the bed. Her hoodie came off, Nick's big hands steady and sure. His fingers edged beneath her tank top, touching the bare skin of her stomach. He gripped her waist firmly as he kissed her again, and then he was urging her to lift up her arms as he tugged off her tank top, tossing it aside. Nick's eyes grew hot as he gazed at her, Kaylee's breasts heaving up and down in her lacy bra. Her curves had filled out since she'd been a teenager, and she could tell he liked what he saw. He'd changed, too. Nick was bigger. Harder. He had strong planes of muscle and a confidence and self-assuredness in his movements. Nick was all man now, and she couldn't get enough of him.

Kaylee gasped in surprise as he lifted her up, his hands beneath her ass as she wrapped her arms and legs around him. "Kaylee," he murmured. "I'll never get enough of you." Their mouths met again, and then they were kissing each other desperately. His stubble rubbed over her skin as his mouth trailed down her neck, and she felt marked by him. Claimed. His musky scent made awareness shoot straight through her, and she knew she'd smell like him tomorrow. She'd be his.

Nick shifted her higher in his arms, impossibly

strong, kissing his way across her cleavage. It was erotic seeing his mouth and the stubble of his jaw at her breasts. Nick was taking what he wanted, and goodness if she didn't want to give it all to him. Kaylee's pussy was throbbing, her panties damp, and she bucked her hips against him, shameless in her need.

"I got you, baby girl," he said, his voice husky. And then Nick was gently laying her down on the bed, his big body coming down atop hers. He was bigger than he'd been years ago, his body harder, chiseled from years of training. She could feel his muscles bunch as he moved, and she was trapped beneath him in bed, exactly where she wanted to be.

Kaylee longed to explore him, feel that powerful strength concealed beneath his clothes. Nick was still fully dressed, and he was kissing his way across her collarbone, trailing down to her breasts once more. He tugged the cups of her bra down, cupping her mounds in his big hands as they spilled over. "You're so damn pretty, Kaylee. Absolutely gorgeous."

Nick's thumbs rubbed over her nipples, and she cried out, not missing his smile. "You were always so sensitive," he murmured, his voice thick. "I love how your body responds to me. It's like it knows you're still mine." She whimpered at the possessiveness of his statement but couldn't deny the truth. A part of her had always been his.

He trailed one thumb around her areola, watching her reaction, before lightly teasing her swollen bud again.

"Nick," she pleaded, her hands wrapping around his wrists. Her fingers didn't even go all the way around, and she felt fragile beneath him and flushed at his attention. He massaged her breasts, smiling at the feel of them in his hands, before finally ducking down. Nick's mouth closed around one nipple as she cried out, and he sucked at her skillfully, a man starved. His tongue was wicked, teasing and laving her swollen bud as she squirmed beneath him. Arousal dampened her folds as she remembered Nick's skills at oral. She might've been young then, but she'd never forgotten the way he'd eagerly pleasure her, making her writhe and cry out his name.

Kaylee whimpered as he bit down gently on one taut bud, but then he was blowing softly on her nipple, easing the sting. Kaylee's hands gripped his head, holding him to her as he gave her other breast the same attention. She could feel his thick erection pressing against her thigh, and her pussy spasmed in anticipation. He'd always been insatiable in bed but also so damn attentive and sweet with her. She'd never come as hard with other boyfriends as she had with Nick, and even now, her body instantly responded to him.

"I'm never going to get enough of you," he murmured, the scruff of his jaw rubbing against her bare breasts. She shivered at his admission, but then Nick kissed his way down her stomach, his hands undoing the button of her jeans.

"You're wearing too many clothes," she protested as he slid down her zipper.

His lips quirked, but those dark eyes met hers. "This is about you right now, baby girl."

And then she was lifting her hips at his encouragement, helping him to push her jeans down. Nick stared at the scrap of fabric covering her pussy, and then his big hand was there, his thumb trailing up her seam through the material. "You're wet," he observed. She flushed as she remembered she was wearing red satin panties. Of course, she'd never expected this night or for him to show up. She'd packed in a hurry when she rushed out of her apartment weeks ago, and she'd only grabbed a few clean things from her suitcase when she'd fled the safehouse. "I can feel you through the satin," he said, watching in awe. "Is all this for me?"

"Nick," she breathed, whimpering his name.

He rubbed her clit through the material, and she moaned, helpless to his touch. Nick lowered his head, slowly kissing his way across her bare stomach, just above her panties. He was teasing her, drawing it out. His mouth reached her hip, and he playfully nipped at her, his thumb still expertly rubbing her swollen clit.

"Don't make me wait," she pleaded.

"I'm gonna taste you," he said, his voice thick as he further spread her thighs. She trembled as she looked at him, this powerful man hovering over her like she was some type of delicacy he couldn't wait to devour.

Tugging the fabric of her panties aside, Nick ducked down, licking her slit. It was erotic seeing his muscular hand at her sex, holding her red satin panties in his grip. And then his mouth was covering her folds, licking and savoring her pussy as she lay before him.

"Nick!" she cried out, pleasure washing over her as he swiped his tongue against her sensitive bundle of nerves.

"You're so fucking sweet, Kaylee. I need all of you." He lifted his head and yanked her panties down, his big hands running down her legs with the motion.

She was grateful he hadn't ripped her panties right off. She only had a few things with her at the motel.

His hands smoothed up her legs again as they trembled, and Nick flashed her a knowing look. Lifting her legs over his strong shoulders, Nick devoured her, his mouth and tongue teasing every fold as she cried out at the sweet pleasure. She felt the stubble from his jaw against her tender flesh as he moved, somehow making the moment even more erotic. Nick was all male, powerful and intense, and his current goal was clearly to drive her absolutely out of her mind. His lips found her clit, and he sucked it into his mouth as she choked out a strangled cry. Two thick fingers penetrated her core, stretching her. Kaylee let out a mewling sound as he moved them in and out, nearly drowning in the pure pleasure he was giving her. Nick's fingers thrust in again, his tongue flicking over her swollen nub. She was helpless in this position, and Nick knew it, clearly eager to drive her wild.

Kaylee was getting higher, closer, her breaths coming in shallow pants as Nick pumped his fingers in and out of her slickened walls. His mouth was hot against her sex, his tongue never letting up, and as the tension continued to build, suddenly Kaylee fisted the sheets and cried out his name, rocketing into one of the strongest orgasms she'd ever experienced.

She was still gasping, her legs tossed over his broad shoulders, as Nick gentled his movements. He didn't completely stop, just softly kissed her folds and nuzzled against her sex as he slowly brought her back down. Her pussy was throbbing, her inner walls still spasming around his thick fingers, and Kaylee swore she saw stars.

"Nick," she breathed, finally meeting his eyes. His mouth was still at her sex, but she could see the satisfaction on his face. He'd always loved pleasuring her, and she'd given herself over to him completely. Nick finally slid his fingers free, sucking off her juices, and then planted a trail of soft kisses down her inner thigh, his big hand flat on her stomach. Kaylee was still at his complete and utter mercy, spread wide before him, but there was nowhere else she wanted to be. He finally eased her legs off his shoulders, and she sank further into the bed, relaxed and sated. Nick had completely wrung her dry.

He was watching her wordlessly, and their exchanged glance said more than words ever could. She was still his after all this time, just as Nick was still hers. Their connection was just as electric as years ago, the chemistry bubbling between them making her blood heat and chest fill with longing. He pressed his lips softly against her stomach, lazily trailing kisses up toward her breasts as he explored. She loved his touches and caresses on her bare skin and couldn't even bring herself to feel embarrassed that he was clothed while she was completely nude. This was Nick. How many nights had they spent years ago doing this exact same thing?

Except today felt like more—so much more.

And she'd never flown as high and come as hard as moments ago.

A sudden rapping on the door had them both freezing, Kaylee's entire body suddenly stiff. Nick hovered above her as if shielding her from the unknown, instantly tense and looking ready to spring into action.

"Fuck," Nick muttered quietly. He was up in an

instant, tossing the sheets over her before moving silently across the room. His hand drew a weapon she hadn't even noticed was there, and she gripped the sheets tightly around her in one hand, hesitating on the bed.

This side of Nick hadn't been there when they were teenagers. He moved swiftly, clearly ready to put himself between her and any potential harm that might come her way. Nick was a former Special Forces soldier, highly trained by the U.S. military, and positively lethal.

Chapter 7

Nick moved toward the door, the taste of Kaylee still on his tongue. Hell. He wanted to devour her—drink up every last drop of her sweet arousal and then kiss his way across her gorgeous, supple body, making her cry out his name again and again. She was beautiful—sexy curves and full breasts, skin as smooth as silk, and a confidence that hadn't been there years ago. The way she'd given herself over to him just now was something he wouldn't take for granted. She was intoxicating.

His cock was still throbbing in his boxer briefs, his erection straining against his jeans, but the sudden knocking on the door had jarred him back into their harsh reality. Kaylee was in danger, and there was no reason for anyone to be knocking on the door of the motel room.

Nick eased the safety off his weapon and kept his arm ready at his side, peering through the peephole. A

-aged woman was standing there in a winter carrying a bag of Chinese takeout. He frowned. k's gaze swiveled toward Kaylee, and he saw that e was already collecting her clothes and hurrying oward the bathroom.

Fuck.

The sight of her naked form was hard to ignore, but he needed to keep her safe.

The bathroom door snicked shut, and the woman knocked on the motel door again. "Peter? I'm back with the Chinese!"

Flicking the safety back on, Nick holstered his weapon. He wouldn't need it to subdue this woman if she did turn out to be a threat. It could be an ambush, he supposed, but no one knew they were here. Certainly, it would've been easier to grab Kaylee earlier when she'd poked her head outside the door than to rush their motel room with him inside.

Nick flipped the latch, opening the door partway. The cold air bit into him, and he blocked the open space with his body so no one could see inside. He was taller than the woman at the door, but he had no idea if anyone else was out there. "You've got the wrong room," he said gruffly.

"What?" she asked, looking startled to see him and taking a step back. "Why are you in my room?"

"I'm not. You're knocking on the wrong door. What room are you looking for?"

"Two-oh-seven."

He cocked his head to the number on the side of their motel room, his eyes never leaving her face. "This is two-oh-six. You're one more down."

She glanced to the numbers and then back at him, realization dawning on her. "Oh, I'm so sorry. I was in a rush and didn't even realize."

"No problem," he said, closing the door before she could say anything else. He locked it again, looking through the peephole to make sure the woman actually left. He watched as she walked away and then heard a door open and close. Nick bit back a curse. He'd gotten carried away earlier, letting his base instincts take over. He needed to keep Kaylee safe tonight, not fuck her into oblivion. Of course, a night with Kaylee would never be just a fuck. Just being in her presence brought up memories and feelings from years ago. Given the current situation, however, and the fact that they'd each be going back to their own lives after this was over, meant he needed to keep his hands to himself. Nick was here to protect Kaylee, not spend endless hours enjoying her delectable body or making her cry out his name.

He walked across the motel room, happy that Kaylee was still in the bathroom. At least she had good survival instincts. He appreciated that she'd let him handle the situation. Nick was former Special Forces. She'd turned to him for help, and she would damn well get it. He wouldn't make any slip-ups from now on, no matter how tempting his beautiful ex might be.

Nick knocked softly on the bathroom door so as not to spook her. "Kaylee? It was a woman who had the wrong room. Everything's okay. You can come out."

She opened the bathroom door, and he took in her flushed cheeks and fearful expression. She'd gone from sexy and sated to terrified in mere moments. "Come 'ere," he muttered, pulling her into his embrace. Nick kissed the top of her head, inhaling her vanilla scent. She practically melted against him, her small body shuddered.

"It's okay. I'm sorry that scared you," he said, running one hand over her back reassuringly, the other cradling the back of her head.

"It's not your fault."

"It's my fault that I was distracted. You're far too tempting." She looked up at him then, flushing slightly, and Nick ducked for one more kiss. He might not be able to make love to her all night for a whole host of reasons, but she was so fucking sweet, he couldn't resist those pretty pink lips. Her body softened against his, and a long dormant part of Nick thrilled that he could make her feel safe and forget the situation.

At that exact moment, Kaylee's stomach rumbled. "Did you eat yet?" Nick asked, suddenly concerned.

She shook her head, still holding onto him. "I haven't had much food all day."

Guilt churned through him. Kaylee had caught a bus out of Omaha this morning, completely terrified. She'd snuck out with only her backpack and probably didn't even have much money with her, if any at all. Nick felt like a jackass for showing up and not asking what she needed. While he'd loved stripping her bare and feeling her orgasm around his fingers and against his mouth, he needed to see to her basic needs. Food. Shelter. Safety. "Why don't I order us some food? I don't want to leave you here alone in the room, so I'll find a local place that delivers. I didn't eat dinner yet either."

She finally pulled away. Nick instantly missed the feel of her in his arms but watched as she crossed the small motel room toward her backpack. "I've got cash with me," Kaylee said as she lifted it up. She unzipp it on the dresser, taking out a plastic grocery bag, and then grabbed her wallet. "I don't want to use my credit cards in case they're looking for me."

"I'll pay for dinner," he said, somewhat frustrated that she even thought he'd let her pay for her own meal. He'd just had her naked and writhing beneath him. If the woman at the door hadn't interrupted, he'd probably be balls deep inside Kaylee right now, making her come again and again. It might've been a bad fucking idea, but he'd always lost all sense when it came to her.

"What'd you buy at the store?" he asked, nodding toward the grocery bag and ignoring the way his cock twitched.

"Peanut butter and crackers. I wasn't sure if I'd have to keep moving, and those seemed easy enough to bring with me."

He stiffened. "Did they provide food and necessities for you at the safehouse?"

Her eyes shot toward his. "They did, but I felt uncomfortable the entire time I was there. I didn't eat much, really, and mostly stayed in my room. I only stopped at the store after I got off the bus here." She shoved the grocery bag into her backpack once more, and he hated that she was already packing up. Kaylee was frightened, but she wasn't on her own anymore. Nick would do everything in his power to keep her safe from here on out.

"I'm sorry that you were scared enough to run, but it was the right thing to do. If these people were impersonating Federal Agents, you're lucky you escaped unharmed."

"I realize that. I hadn't given them any reason to

. me, but as the days ticked by and they didn't me anything, I knew something was very wrong."

"Let's order some dinner, and then I'll reach out to my teammates. They were already running the plate of the car following me earlier, but now that you've given me a name, that'll help immensely. My guys can look into some of the other people working at Offutt as well."

"They can access that?" she asked doubtfully.

Nick leveled her with a look. "You'd be surprised with what we have access to. Our IT guys are the best. West can get into anything."

"Can he figure out who the men were at my apartment?"

"The ones who took you to the safehouse?" Nick asked.

Kaylee worried her lip, nodding. "Yeah. They knew exactly where I lived, but like I said, they never showed any identification to me."

Nick pulled his phone from his pocket, swiping the screen. "Tell me the date and approximate time this happened. You don't have one of those doorbell cameras, right? I don't remember seeing one."

"No," she said, shaking her head. "There are multiple cameras around the apartment complex though."

"I figured as much. West should be able to access the surveillance footage from when the men came to your place. Maybe West can get a visual on whoever was in the vehicle following me tonight as well." He thumbed the details into a text message as Kaylee gave him an approximate time and date. "There," he said after shooting off the message. "I'll give the team a call after we eat, but that gives them something to start working on."

He crossed over to Kaylee and searched online for a local restaurant that delivered, looking at the options with her. It felt so damn right having her standing there at his side, Nick almost didn't know what to make of it. He'd just stripped her bare and pleasured her, and now they were ordering dinner like nothing had happened. But how many nights had exactly that happened—they'd made love, laughed, eaten meals, and more. He'd missed this type of closeness with another person. Sometimes the moments after intimacy could be awkward, but clearly, he'd been with the wrong women. It was never that way with her. When Kaylee was near, it was like his life simply clicked into place.

After Nick placed their order, Kaylee shot him a worried look. "What is it?" he asked, frowning.

"Is your boss going to be okay with this? I feel like I'm causing a lot of trouble for everyone. I just didn't know who else to turn to or who I could trust."

"You can trust me," he assured her.

"I know that, but now your friends are helping me, too. I don't want your boss to get mad."

Nick's lips quirked, his eyes trailing over her face. She was so damn sweet it practically hurt, but it meant a lot that she seemed worried about him, too. Kaylee wasn't the type of woman to take advantage of someone. She'd always been genuine, with smarts he admired and an infectious giggle that made him smile. Nick liked to joke around but had always been more intense than her. Kaylee had always been goodness and light.

As his gaze slid downward, his heart thudded in his chest. Kaylee also had a body he craved, a kiss that made his blood heat, making his own body pulse with energy and awareness. He didn't think he'd ever stop wanting her, and it would be hell to have to let her go when this was over.

His eyes finally met hers once again. "It's not a problem. My boss is the one that sent me."

Chapter 8

Kaylee sat beside Nick in his rental car the following morning, feeling unsettled. Nick's words had churned in her mind all night: "My boss is the one who sent me." That's what this was all about. She was a job. Yes, they had a past, and the fire between them burned even hotter than it had years ago. The reality of the situation was that this was Nick's life now. He worked for a security company. He was on a Black Ops Team. Her insides twisted as she wondered how many other women he'd slept with—women he was tasked to protect. Surely every woman he came across didn't fall into bed with him as quickly as she had, but there must have been others. Nick was attentive and protective, not to mention hot as hell.

Embarrassment washed over her as she recalled last night. He'd tried to slow things down, and she'd practically begged him to take her. She bit her lip, glancing out the window as the trees flew by. After they'd eaten dinner, he'd called some of his team and briefed them on the situation. The license plate of the car tailing Nick had come back as stolen, giving them no helpful information on the men who'd been inside. Kaylee and Nick had gone to bed shortly after that, planning to get an early start today.

She'd flushed as she'd seen him come out of the bathroom in boxers and a tee shirt last night. Nick hadn't made things awkward though. He'd simply climbed into bed and wrapped himself around Kaylee, holding her close. She hadn't begged him to kiss or undress her again. He hadn't tried to either. Nick holding her as she slept felt intimate in a different way, and she didn't even know what to make of the conflicting feelings coursing through her.

"What are you thinking so hard about?" Nick asked quietly. He flipped on the turn signal, taking the next exit. They'd decided to drive the several hours back to Omaha, and Nick's boss had arranged for a private jet back to New York. She was nervous about someone finding her before then, but Nick had assured Kaylee that he'd keep her safe. She didn't doubt that he'd protect her physically, but as for her heart? She'd have to guard that more carefully.

"I'm just nervous," she said truthfully.

She felt Nick's eyes on her but didn't look over at him. When his gaze returned to the road, it was a relief. "You've been quiet since last night," he observed.

Kaylee let out a soft sigh. "I'm scared. I haven't been home in a month, Nick. And things between us? We got carried away last night," she said softly, feeling her cheeks heat.

Nick reached over and took her hand, and she

instantly felt her heartbeat slow. He'd always been able to soothe her with a simple touch. "I apologize for taking advantage of you like that. You were scared and vulnerable. I should never have stripped you bare and—"

She looked over at him in surprise. "You think that's what this is about?" she interrupted. "You think that I'm mad at you?"

"You've been quiet ever since the woman knocked on the door when we were in bed together."

"I'm embarrassed," she admitted softly. "You probably protect other women all the time and I'm just—"

"There's no one else, Kaylee," he said, his deep voice doing something funny to her insides. "Sure, I've rescued other women over the years, but do I spend the night in their hotel room? Hold them close while I sleep because I can't stand the thought of being apart? Negative. Everything has always been different with you."

She felt her eyes welling with tears and glanced down at their joined hands. "You said your boss sent you, Nick."

He gripped her hand tighter, his thumb rubbing over her skin. "You think I don't want to be here? Jett told me to come so I'd get my head out of my ass. I've been worried about you ever since I got your text. Ask my teammates when you meet them. They all know about you. Sure, it's been years since we were a couple, but when I thought you were in trouble? Hell. There's nothing I wouldn't do to get to you."

She looked over at him in surprise, his admission stunning her.

"Nick," she said softly.

"I let you go all those years ago so you'd be free to do what you wanted and be happy in life. We were both so damn young."

"Timing is everything," she said, a sudden feeling of regret churning through her.

"We did what was right at the time. I never thought circumstances would lead me right back to your door, but here we are. I've spent my career chasing bad guys, ridding the world of evil men. If there are traitors stealing classified information at Offutt who are now out to get you because you were the lone witness, they have no idea who they're dealing with. I'm better-suited to protect you than anyone, and I'll damn well do it. I swear nothing will happen to you while you're under my protection."

"And after that?" she asked.

He didn't answer, and Kaylee knew he was thinking the same thing that she was. They lived separate lives. Even though they'd picked up like a single day hadn't passed, they were removed from their real lives at the moment. She'd go back to Omaha. He'd return to New York. The sudden ache in her chest was surprising. She wasn't supposed to see Nick again, spend the night in his arms, so why did she suddenly long for what she'd given up all those years ago? The life she'd missed out on seemed to be dangling right in front of her. Nick was here, solid and strong and real.

"We'll figure it out," he finally said.

He kept hold of her hand as he drove, but Kaylee knew in her heart he'd disappear when this was all over. He'd left her behind once before, even though the decision had been mutual. They each had their own separate lives now.

That didn't mean she wouldn't always wonder what she'd missed out on.

***

Five hours later, Nick was leading her off the private jet. One of his teammates was there to greet them, and Kaylee didn't miss his assessing gaze as he walked toward them. The guy was muscular, with dark hair and a short beard. As the sun peeked out from behind the clouds, he slid his sunglasses on. Somehow, he looked even harder than Nick. He was bigger, more muscular, but this man had been through something, no doubt. He was alert in a way Nick wasn't. The "fuck-off" vibes radiating off his large frame let her know not to ask any questions. He might not hurt her, but he also wasn't about to sit down for a heart-to-heart either.

"Kaylee, this is Gray," Nick said as the man stopped in front of them. "We served together as Deltas and work together now at Shadow Security."

Gray held out a hand, and it engulfed her own. She resisted the urge to press closer to Nick. Kaylee worked with military men and macho types on base. She wouldn't let this one intimidate her. She noticed a tattoo peeking out from beneath his short sleeves. It was freezing cold outside, but he didn't seem to notice. Kaylee had one of Nick's big sweatshirts on over her own clothes, giving her some extra warmth. If Gray noticed that she was wearing Nick's things, he didn't comment on it. She doubted much got past him though. His hand was rough, but he was gentle as he shook hers. "I've heard a lot about you," Gray said, his voice a deep timbre. "I wish we were meeting under better circumstances."

"Likewise," she agreed. "You served with Nick?"

"Guilty as charged," he quipped "Can't get rid of the guy now."

"Asshole," Nick muttered, but there wasn't any heat in his tone. She was surprised Gray had made a joke at all. He seemed nothing but gruff and serious, but maybe he was just trying to make her feel more comfortable. Nick's gaze landed on Kaylee again. "Gray's going to drop us off at my place. I hope that's okay. We could get you a hotel room, but I'd rather have eyes on you to make sure you're safe."

"Of course," she said, feeling flustered as Gray's lips quirked. His expression seemed all too knowing. She was positive Nick hadn't told him what went on between them last night, but the men must all realize she was an ex-girlfriend. And what did Gray mean by saying he'd heard a lot about her?

"After we get you settled, we'll head over to Shadow Security," Nick continued. "West and his guys have some info for us."

"Really?" she asked.

Nick nodded. "I don't know what they found out yet, only that they're eager to speak with us. I believe they're hoping you can provide some additional information as well. We'd like to know who else may be involved in this so they can dig deeper."

"We should head straight there," Kaylee said.

"Whatever you prefer," Nick assured her. "We can go there first and then to my place afterwards. One of the guys will have to give us a lift, since I don't have my car. Lena, my boss's assistant, is getting some things for you. Clothes. Extra toiletries. That type of stuff. We'll make sure you have what you need while you're staying here in New York."

"Oh, wow. She didn't have to do all that."

"She doesn't mind," Gray said matter-of-factly. Kaylee's eyes shifted to him, and she wondered how familiar he was with his boss's hired hand.

"He's right," Nick said with a shrug. "Jett pays her well. Lena used to handle everything for him before he got married—work-related stuff, errands, cooking."

"Jett's even had her purchase Anna a gift or two," Gray said, and she could see him biting back a smile. Before she could ask him what that was about, he turned, heading toward his truck. Kaylee watched him quizzically. For such a stern, macho guy, he seemed to have a soft spot for this woman.

"Do I even want to know what type of gifts she was buying for this Anna person?"

Nick chuckled. "I can only imagine. Anna's a firecracker. After the night she and the boss met, she basically moved in with him and never left. They have a baby now plus another on the way. They just got married in December," he added.

"Guess they don't waste any time," Kaylee joked, and she and Nick began moving across the tarmac toward the parking lot. Gray hadn't turned around once, just assumed they'd follow. He seemed to be giving them a moment alone as well, which she appreciated. Her entire life had flipped on its side in the past twenty-four hours. The bus ride to the motel. Nick showing up in Nebraska. His hands and mouth on her….

She could feel herself flushing again.

Nick wrapped his arm around her shoulders,

pulling her close. His lips pressed against the top of her head, and she felt her body instinctively relaxing into him. It felt good to be at his side. Safe. "We're gonna figure this out," he promised.

"I hope so. You don't want me rooming with you for the rest of your life," she said, attempting a weak joke.

"I don't know. Last night worked out pretty well for a shitty motel. But if you were living with me, Kaylee?" She looked up at him as she waited for him to finish, shocked by the intensity in his eyes. "We'd be a hell of a lot more than just roommates."

Chapter 9

Nick glanced back at Kaylee, who was clutching her hands together nervously in the double cab of Gray's truck. She was biting her lip, looking out the window, her backpack and Nick's duffle bag stashed on the empty seat beside her. The men had been talking quietly on the drive to headquarters. Nick had tried to explain a little about the area to Kaylee but could tell she was overwhelmed and stressed, so he gave her some space to sort out her thoughts—as much as he could, anyway, given that they were all together in the pickup.

"Jett called for a briefing in an hour," Gray said. "West will be there to fill the team in."

Nick huffed out a breath. "I'm going to find him beforehand. I want to know if they figured out who those assholes were on my tail last night."

"Think you were made?"

"No doubt they got photos. Whether or not they

can ID me depends on who exactly they were. I was at Kaylee's apartment door, key in hand, ready to enter when she called me."

Gray's eyes moved to the rearview mirror for a beat, and Kaylee shifted in the backseat. She was quiet but clearly listening.

Nick cleared his throat. "After I stopped by her parents' place—shit. That reminds me," he said, looking back toward Kaylee again. "Jett got a message to your family, letting your mom know that you're okay and with me. We don't want to call them on an open line, but you'll be able to speak with them yourself when we're at headquarters."

"Oh good," she said, letting out a sigh of relief. "It's been a month since we've spoken."

"I know she'll be happy to hear from you." Nick watched her for a beat, studying Kaylee as she nodded, and then his gaze landed on his buddy again. She made a soft sniffling sound in the backseat, and his chest clenched. She'd been through a hell of a lot, and he was up front with Gray. He wished he'd sat beside her. Gray might've given him shit, but this was Kaylee. He didn't give a fuck what his friends thought.

"Maybe they weren't close enough to get a clear photo of you."

"Hopefully not," Nick agreed. "Not that they'd be able to learn much."

"Life in the shadows has its perks," Gray muttered.

Nick frowned. His buddy wasn't wrong. When they'd been Deltas, it's not like their names and faces had been plastered all over the Internet. Likewise, Shadow Security kept things under wraps. It was why

Kaylee had no clue how he'd spent the past few years. Thankfully, she had reached out to him anyway last month, assuming he was a bodyguard. He hated to think what would've happened if anyone found Kaylee holed up in that motel room alone. The thought of anyone touching or hurting her made his blood boil.

Nick's phone buzzed just then, and he lifted it to his ear. "Nick here."

"It's West," his friend said in a clipped tone.

"We're on our way to headquarters right now. What's wrong?" Nick asked, glancing out the window. There was no privacy in the cab of the truck, but he knew West wouldn't have called if it wasn't important.

"Someone broke into Kaylee's apartment this afternoon. The place was completely ransacked. The police and fire department are both there right now. Multiple emergency vehicles are at the scene."

"Shit," Nick spat out, clutching his phone more tightly. "They set it on fire?"

"Yes," West said, his voice grim. "I was monitoring things in Omaha before you went wheels up earlier. I wanted to make sure no trouble was headed your way. This just happened about an hour ago."

"What's the extent of the damage?"

"Unknown. I'll reach out to some contacts to see what else I can find out. I can always listen in on the police scanners as well."

"Appreciate you letting me know," Nick said. Irritation roiled through him. How dare someone go to Kaylee's home, destroying her property. What if she'd been inside when the intruders had shown up?

Would they have hurt her? Taken her? Fear washed over him. Nick wasn't a man who cowered in the face of danger, but the thought of any harm coming to Kaylee made him feel physically sick.

"We'll talk more when you get here," West said. "I've got additional updates.

"Roger that. ETA is ten minutes."

"Gotcha. See you soon."

Nick muttered a curse as he ended the call. He appreciated West giving him a head's up. Kaylee would be devasted to learn her place had been broken into and set ablaze. He didn't want to have to give her the bad news, but they'd be meeting with the rest of the team soon. It would be worse for her to find out in front of everyone.

"What's wrong?" Kaylee asked, her green eyes wide as he looked back at her once more. Nick took a moment to drink her in, mentally cataloguing every feature. Her lips had parted, and her brown hair hung down to her shoulders, soft and shiny. He'd watched her get ready this morning at the motel, and something primal within him had stirred. Nick didn't want another man having those quiet moments with her—holding her close at night, waking up together each morning. He might want to make love to her more than he wanted his next breath, but it was more than that. He wanted the right to always have her by his side.

"Nick?" she asked.

He blinked, dragging his eyes back to her face. "There's been a complication," Nick said, and Gray's head swiveled his way. Nick cleared his throat. "That was West, our IT guy, who called just now. He was monitoring things in Omaha and told me there was a break-in and fire at your apartment."

Kaylee gasped, her lower-lip wobbling. "A fire? When?" she asked.

"This afternoon. West didn't give me many other details or know the extent of the damage yet, but he'll find out more and fill us in when we get there. I'm sorry," he said, meeting her eyes. "I didn't want you to find out about it in front of everyone else. It seems that you were targeted."

She didn't answer, and as she swallowed, Nick didn't miss the sheen of wetness in her eyes.

"Your parents already know that you're okay," he reminded her. "If anyone else thinks you were in the apartment, well, maybe that's a good thing. It kills me that they went to your home, destroying your property, but it might buy us some additional time."

"They were looking for me."

"They were, and I'm so sorry about that. Maybe my going there yesterday made them think you'd return. The timing was shit as far as you leaving the safehouse the day I arrived in Omaha, but what's done is done. I'm not sure why it'd be set on fire unless they believed someone was inside."

"That's fucked up," Gray muttered. "But if they broke into her place, they should've easily been able to figure out no one was home."

"True. And West said her place was ransacked. Shit. I didn't even think to ask him if they caught the perps." He grabbed his phone and thumbed a text.

Nick: They catch the intruders?

West: Negative. One of the neighbors called the police. The perps weren't very subtle about it. Someone literally busted down her door.

He clenched his fist. Once they realized Kaylee

had disappeared from the safehouse, her apartment was one of the first places they'd check. They'd been watching the place yesterday, and he'd shown up, throwing them off. Had someone watched her building all night and then moved in?

Nick: What about the cameras at her apartment complex?

West: Already running through the footage.

"Well?" Gray asked as Nick set his phone back down.

"They got away. West is reviewing the surveillance camera footage."

"Well fuck," Gray said, and to Nick's surprise, Kaylee giggled in the backseat.

"That's an understatement," she said.

Gray's lips quirked, and he briefly met her gaze in the rearview mirror. "It was, but we'll get the bastards behind it. Nick is one of the best men I know, and you'll be safe staying with him."

Ten minutes later, they were on the secluded, tree-lined road leading to headquarters. Jett liked the surrounding forest for security and privacy, and Nick appreciated that more than ever now that Kaylee was here. They pulled through the gated entrance, the large building looming in front of them. A minute later, Nick hopped out of the passenger seat and was taking Kaylee's hand, helping her out of the truck. His other hand landed on her waist, and he didn't miss the slight hitch of her breath. Nick held her securely as she climbed down, the blush spreading across her cheeks reminding him of the way she flushed beneath him last night. He might hate that she was in danger, but he loved how Kaylee always responded to his touch. As innocent as this gesture had been, it was like her body knew she was made to be his.

"What about our stuff?" she asked, glancing back as Gray shut the door.

Gray glanced at their joined hands but didn't comment on it. "You can leave it here. I'll give you guys a lift to Nick's place, assuming that's where you're staying." Irritation roiled through Nick, but he couldn't deny he appreciated Gray being willing to do what Kaylee wanted. If she changed her mind about staying with him, no one would force her to. Hell. He'd sleep outside her hotel room door if that's what he needed to do in order to protect her.

"Okay. I guess it's safe to leave in the truck," she said, glancing to the perimeter fence and cameras surrounding the property.

"Safest place it can be," Nick said, leading her toward the building. "Jett has security monitoring the premises. No one is getting in who doesn't belong here."

Nick caught his and Kaylee's reflection in the glass as they walked to the front door, and something in his chest stirred. Never in a million years had he imagined bringing his ex here. All the different parts of his life felt like they were colliding, but surprisingly, he didn't hate it. He and Kaylee weren't fresh-faced teenagers anymore. It felt right having her hand in his, bringing her to the job he was damn proud of, introducing her to his teammates. He'd worked hard to get where he was in life, but something had been missing.

He'd never had anyone to share it with before.

For the first time, he was beginning to see why most of his friends had fallen head-over-heels for their women. Aside from Nick and Gray, everyone else was part of a couple. And he was beginning to have his doubts about Gray. His buddy seemed to pay more attention to Lena than he'd realized before.

Gray swiped his badge, holding open the doors for them.

Clara glanced up from where she sat behind the receptionist's desk as they walked in, and her eyes widened as she saw Nick, her gaze moving between him and Kaylee. Before she could say anything, Anna came out from the secure area, her blonde hair swishing behind her. "You're back!" she said, rushing over to greet them. She was teetering in high heels despite the fact that she was several months pregnant, and her wrap dress swirled around her legs, the bracelets on her arm jangling. Nick got an eyeful of cleavage as she adjusted her dress and quickly averted his gaze.

"You must be Kaylee. I'm so glad that you're okay!" Anna exclaimed, drawing her in for a hug. "Nick, you didn't tell us how pretty she is. I would kill for those green eyes."

"Thanks," Kaylee said, clearly taken aback by Anna's exuberance.

"Jett's on his way," Anna continued. "He's just finishing up something with Lena. I'm heading out soon myself. I've been part-time since having the boss's baby," she told Kaylee. "We're married, so it's okay," she added with a wink.

Nick resisted the urge to groan. Anna was something else. While he didn't usually mind her exuberance, Kaylee was scared and upset. Of course, Anna didn't know about the break-in and fire. She helped out with admin tasks and kept headquarters running smoothly but wouldn't be privy to conversations about potential operations. Nick hated that Kaylee was now a "job" to his teammates, but he'd be damned if he let anyone hurt her. Having the Shadow Ops Team at her back would settle the issues stemming from Offutt sooner rather than later.

In the back of his mind, Nick wondered what Kaylee's employer thought of her absence. She might have been working on base, but her company was contracting with DEA. Had all of them simply gone along with her disappearance? Were they kept in the dark about it? Or was there a possibility even more people were involved than those already on his radar?

"Oh, here they come!" Anna trilled. "I hear my hubby's voice," she added, smiling.

Gray's eyes were already on the door, and a beat later, Jett and his assistant walked out, Sam close behind them. Lena looked ready to leave for the day, her coat on and designer purse slung over her shoulder. She always looked sophisticated and put-together, although she wasn't flashy in the way that Anna was. Lena didn't even seem to notice the way Gray was watching her, and she stopped by the receptionist's desk as Jett and Sam headed straight toward them.

"I told you I didn't want to see you in the office today," Jett quipped as he walked over. Kaylee shrunk back slightly into Nick, and Sam chuckled.

"He's just yanking Nick's chain," Sam said, his eyes sparking with amusement "The boss told him to go find you. And here you are," he said with a shit-eating grin. "I'm Sam," he added, holding out his hand.

"Kaylee," she responded softly, looking between him and Jett.

"Don't be an ass," Nick warned, and Sam dropped

Kaylee's hand, still grinning.

"I'm Jett," their boss said, holding out his hand to Kaylee. "I'm glad Nick was able to locate you, although it sounds like the circumstances have been less than ideal. West just gave me the update about your apartment, and while I'm sorry you were targeted, I'm thankful you're okay. I trust you'll be interested to learn what else my IT guys have found out. Nick can show you around later if you'd like, but we'll be briefing shortly to discuss the situation."

"Okay. Thank you. I hope it's not an inconvenience for you to have me here."

"An inconvenience? Nonsense. I need my best sniper to have his head in the game. He's been worried about you all month," Jett said seriously. "And it sounds like he had just cause to be concerned. I'm glad he brought you back with him. Nick will keep you safe," he added, his gaze intense as he watched her.

"These guys are the best," Anna promised.

"I see you've already met my better-half," Jett quipped, his mood lightening. Anna smiled sweetly and snuggled up against Jett, and Nick could see Kaylee relaxing slightly. Jett's sharp gaze and assertive personality could be intimidating to those who didn't know him. Hell. He could scare the shit out of men he did know. Anna softened him in many ways, and even now, Jett wrapped his arm around his wife, pressing a kiss to her temple.

The door from the basement opened just then, and Luke and Ford walked in. "You work fast," Ford said, but his lips quirked. More introductions were made, and unable to resist, Nick wrapped his arm around Kaylee's shoulders.

"I hate to draw this gathering to a close, but we should move to the conference room," Jett told the team. "Aside from the leak of classified information stemming from Offutt, which will have its own repercussions, Ms. Thomas is in grave danger."

Chapter 10

Kaylee sank down into the chair Nick pulled out for her in the sleek, modern conference room, her entire body tense. She could feel the eyes of Nick's friends on her. They weren't accusatory or suspicious, just curious. Clearly, Nick with a woman at his side was a rarity. Although she was surprised, she had to admit that thought made warmth wash over her. Even when she and Nick went their separate ways after this was over, which they no doubt would, she could leave knowing she wasn't just another notch on his bedpost.

Not that she'd be jumping into bed with him. Yesterday at the motel had been a moment of weakness. They might both still be attracted to one another, but they also each knew how this would end.

Didn't they?

Nick dragged out the chair beside her and sank down, his athletic, lean body folding into the seat. He was close enough that she could smell his musky scent, and that made her relax a small degree. She was used to briefings at Offutt, but this was different in a thousand ways. It was personal, and it affected her entire life and career.

Jett moved to the front of the room, and then a man she hadn't met yet appeared, papers in hand. While they conferred quietly, Nick nodded to a secure phone on the table. "After the briefing, you can call your family. Unless you'd rather do so right now? I can take you to my office."

She searched his gaze, noting the sincerity there. If she wanted, he'd get her out of here. Despite her uncertainty, she had to admit that Nick seemed to have her best interests at heart. Determined to move forward with the briefing, she shook her head. "No. I'd rather tell your friends everything I know first. The more information they have, the quicker this will be over, right?"

"Right," he agreed. Nick reached over and squeezed her hand, and she loved the feel of his muscular hand holding her own. Flushing, she realized the other men were watching them. Nick's thumb ran over her knuckles, and she resisted the urge to shiver at his touch.

One of his teammates, Luke, suddenly bit back a curse.

"What's wrong?" Nick immediately asked.

Luke flipped the laptop he was looking at shut. "The apartment fire in Omaha is on their local news." The rest of the men stirred around her, shooting sympathetic looks in Nick's and her direction. "It doesn't seem big enough to draw that much attention so quickly, but for some reason, multiple camera crews are stationed there, reporting on it."

Nick bristled beside her.

"Maybe they were tipped off," Ford surmised.

"It's possible," Luke agreed.

"I don't like it," Nick said. "Anything drawing more attention to Kaylee is bad news, no pun intended."

"My disappearance hasn't been on the news though," she added. "I did Internet searches yesterday. Don't worry, I was careful, using a private browser," she added.

"Whoever started the fire could've notified the media," Ford said. "I hate to say it, but your 'disappearance' might be a story soon, too."

Kaylee frowned, knowing he was right. Before any of the men could respond, Jett was bringing the room to attention. "The information Ms. Thomas has shared with our team is concerning. As everyone is aware, she was working at Offutt Air Force Base on a contract for DEA. One evening approximately a month ago, Ms. Thomas witnessed Colonel Mike Cornwell, an officer stationed at Offutt, and a currently unidentified woman from Human Resources stealing classified information when she unexpectedly returned to her office. Ms. Thomas was approached by several men claiming to be Federal Agents approximately an hour later at her apartment building. They indicated she was a key witness to an ongoing espionage case. Rather than interviewing her on base or taking a statement, they escorted her to an alleged safehouse, where she was held for nearly one month."

"This place was located in Omaha?" Luke asked, frowning.

"Yes," Kaylee said with a nod. "It wasn't far from my apartment, maybe thirty minutes or so. I was scared about what I'd just witnessed. I had no idea what they were photographing, but I was shocked to even have seen something like that. As everyone in this room is no doubt aware, they shouldn't have had cameras in the secure area. I recognized Colonel Cornwell but didn't even know his name at the time." Kaylee continued, further explaining to Nick's teammates what had happened that night. "The people holding me at the safehouse wouldn't provide me with any updates, and I began to grow suspicious. I finally snuck out yesterday morning through a window and took a bus out of town."

"You were held there against your will?" Gray asked. He shot Nick a look.

Nick huffed out a breath, seeming annoyed on her behalf. "She wasn't held hostage, but she was kept there under the premise of it being for her own safety and instructed not to leave or make contact with anyone. She didn't have her phone. While Kaylee did have a laptop, she wasn't connected to any WiFi. We're doubting the legitimacy of the men who took her there. She was never interviewed, never given a timeline as to when she'd testify, and she never provided even a brief statement to investigators."

"They wanted me out of the picture," Kaylee said. "If I couldn't report what had happened, they could get away with it."

Gray cleared his throat. "Excuse me for being blunt, but why would they waste their time holding you there? If they wanted you out of the picture to avoid reporting what had happened, there are other ways to make you disappear."

Kaylee felt Nick stiffen beside her.

"Why didn't they kill me?" she asked, suddenly feeling numb. "I don't think they were real FBI Agents, but they probably worked for the government in some capacity. I can only assume covering up a murder wasn't something they wanted to deal with. Plus, they likely were being paid to hold me there."

"It would draw more attention to the situation if Kaylee disappeared for good," Jett said. "We're assuming they'd let Kaylee return at some point but convince her not to talk via one means or another."

"Blackmail?" Sam wondered.

"I don't think we can rule anything out," Jett said.

Kaylee sucked in a breath. "They didn't have a plan. I'm sure Colonel Cornwell and the woman from HR didn't expect anyone to catch them that night. The entire office was empty. I'm a graphic designer but don't work on current issues. Other offices have reports that are immediately disseminated to the wider military, intelligence, and law enforcement community. My office isn't one that's staffed twenty-four-seven. Other areas of the building would've been teeming with people."

"They went where they knew they'd have privacy," Sam said.

"Exactly," Kaylee agreed. "They were in an office, um—" She cut off, feeling her face turn red. She might be a grown woman, but somehow explaining what she'd seen and heard to a roomful of gruff, former military men made her feel like a shy teenager.

"They were having sex," Nick said. "And then Kaylee witnessed the woman photographing the documents after they were done."

Sam crossed his arms, eyeing them. "This was a

classified area of the building, right? Assuming they had to badge in to enter, there'd be a record of it."

"And a record of Kaylee," Nick pointed out.

She glanced at him, thinking. "What if they were planning to blackmail me? Or somehow tie me to the incident? I never went into my office on Sunday nights, and now I'll be electronically fingerprinted as having been there as well. Maybe they held me for a month to somehow link me to all of it in additional ways." She closed her eyes, frustrated, and felt Nick shifting beside her, taking her hand again. "I should've called security right then, not left the building."

"You were scared and didn't know what to do," Nick said, his voice calm. "No one knows how they'll react in that type of situation. Didn't the guy threaten you?"

"Sort of," she said, trying to fight back the tears she felt coming on.

The man who'd been conferring with Jett earlier moved to the front of the room and introduced himself. "The guys all know me already, but I'm West. I'm head of the IT department here at Shadow Security. I ran a background check as well as some additional searches on the dark Web about Colonel Cornwell," he said. "It appears he's had multiple affairs in the past and is currently separated from his wife."

Kaylee frowned. "I remember the woman from HR saying his wife didn't know he was there. He seemed, um, quite happy with her attention. They were in an office with a door open, so I could hear everything."

"He probably hasn't let anyone know that he's

separated," Nick said.

"He had plenty of reasons not to be caught. He didn't want to lose his job or his pussy," Sam spat out.

Jett leveled him with a look, but Kaylee filled with anger. Sam was right. Cornwell was in it for money and sex. That was all. Kaylee had simply been in the way. Because she was a witness of his misdeeds, she'd been effectively silenced, whisked away from it all until he could determine how to deal with her.

"They couldn't have held Kaylee in that safehouse forever," Nick said, his voice hard.

"I still don't understand what happened at my apartment today," she said, hating the way her voice wobbled. "Maybe they were looking for me or planting some fake evidence, but then why set it on fire?"

"They were covering up something," Nick said. "Whatever they did, maybe it didn't go as planned."

"We need to find out exactly who those men were that took Kaylee," Ford said, leaning forward and resting his forearms on the table. "Identifying them is crucial. They've got to be associated with Cornwell. Either he ordered her to be brought to the supposed safehouse or the woman from HR did."

"They could've been hired guns," Luke said.

"We don't know that," Nick ground out. He was pulsing with anger, and Kaylee wasn't sure what to make of it. She reached over, running her hand over his forearm. He looked down at the table and huffed out a breath.

"I'm fine," she said, sensing his anger was purely on her behalf. "I left the safehouse, and they have absolutely no idea where I am right now." He nodded but didn't say anything.

"We're pulling all surveillance footage from your apartment complex and the surrounding streets," West said. "If we can ID these guys, I can pull background info on them as well. It'll help tie this entire investigation together."

"What about Colonel Cornwell?" Kaylee asked. "Should I report what I saw now that I'm somewhere safe and have access to a phone? I can reach out to our Security Information Officer."

Jett looked toward her, his face grim, and Kaylee felt her heart drop. "The Security Information Officer was found dead this morning."

Chapter 11

"Are you okay?" Nick asked later that evening, walking across his living room toward Kaylee. She sat quietly on the sofa, his big sweatshirt engulfing her much-smaller frame. Something inside his chest twisted at the sight of her there in his home, wearing his clothes. She looked so damn scared and fragile, and while he hated the situation she'd been put in, he didn't regret having her here. She'd been withdrawn ever since Jett's revelation, and he'd do whatever it took to make her feel safe and secure.

As he moved closer, Nick felt something settle inside him, like she was meant to be here, in his home, in his life.

Kaylee swallowed as she met his gaze. "I just can't believe any of this. They really killed him?"

Nick frowned. "Yes. Someone must've gone to him and reported the incident—or a similar one. It can't be a damn coincidence that the day you left the safehouse, he ends up a violent statistic."

She worried her lip, the fear in her eyes evident. "But who else knew about it? Did they think I went straight to him yesterday? Even if they took him out of the picture, so to speak, he's not exactly the only security officer out there. I could've reported the incident to any number of people."

Nick sank down beside her, his hand landed on her denim-clad thigh. He squeezed gently, trying to reassure her. "I wish I knew the answer to that. Someone else could've witnessed something they shouldn't have. Hell, maybe once you disappeared yesterday morning, one of the men holding you went to him, hoping to save their own ass. I assume he'd document whatever he was told, however, so the paper trail should still be there. Or electronic trail," he added as an afterthought. "I doubt that was the first time they were secretly photographing classified materials or going at it like rabbits in an empty office. If they really wanted to keep their affair a secret, they should've gotten a damn hotel room—and not sworn an oath to their country," he added, his voice hardening.

"All of it is sick and twisted," Kaylee said with a shudder.

"It is. People do crazy things based on greed and infatuation. She wanted classified materials. He wanted sex with a much-younger woman."

"I wonder what she photographed," Kaylee murmured.

"West is trying to determine that," Nick assured her. "He's attempting to hack into some of their secure databases to see what Cornwell has been accessing."

"Is that safe or even legal?" Kaylee asked, looking concerned.

"We don't do things the way the military does," Nick admitted. "Black Ops Team, remember? Jett's already been in contact with some of the higher-ups at Offutt. He's got connections all over the world. They're aware of what we're investigating."

"Wait, so they're already reviewing this incident, too?"

Nick nodded. "If not now, they will be ASAP. Especially now that a man has turned up dead. The wheels have already been set in motion. We'll do our part as well, just to ensure nothing is overlooked. We don't typically step in when we're not tasked to do so, but there have been other instances like this when we're protecting our own."

"But I'm not yours," Kaylee said, looking flustered as she glanced down at Nick's hand on her thigh.

He left it there. It was a possessive gesture just as much as it was meant to soothe her. Kaylee might not know it yet, but she was his. He'd been a fool to walk away all those years ago. Sure, they'd been young, but now that she was back in his life and he'd once again felt the chemistry between them, he wasn't going to let her get away again. If she truly didn't want a relationship with him, that was one thing. But her flushes and responses to him, the way her breath hitched when he was close…. her body told another story. She might be skittish and scared at the moment, but the situation wouldn't drag on forever. They'd get the men responsible for detaining her. Arrest Cornwell and the woman from HR.

And after that?

He'd do whatever he could to prove he wasn't the

young, dumb kid he'd once been. He'd do whatever it took to make her his.

"Lena dropped off some things for you," Nick said, nodding toward two shopping bags near the front door. "Clothes, a winter coat, and some other stuff."

"Oh," Kaylee said, seemingly surprised by the change in topic. "You'll have to thank her for me."

Nick nodded, not saying anything else. He absentmindedly caressed her thigh again, and Kaylee leaned into him, her vanilla scent filling the air. He closed his eyes for a beat as her head leaned against his shoulder, absorbing the feel of her at his side. Nick was exhausted, both physically and mentally. As a sniper, he was used to lying in wait. This type of waiting, however, wasn't something he was accustomed to. This wasn't just any mission. Someone he cared for was in danger. His entire body tensed as he thought the situation over. It felt like they were just waiting for the other shoe to drop. This wasn't any old mission, taking out terrorists and rescuing complete strangers. This was Kaylee.

Nick wasn't scared when he deployed on ops, his training having prepared him, the adrenaline coursing through his veins keeping him alert. Sharp. The team moved in with multiple backup plans, their ops well-executed maneuvers.

But at the moment? He felt fucking helpless. Nick was mad as hell that someone had been to Kaylee's apartment. They'd kept her in a safehouse for a month and were no doubt searching for her now. She might have escaped, but Nick knew they were coming. If his team didn't discover who the men were who'd held her, bringing them to justice, he had no doubt they'd be waiting for Kaylee. He'd never feel safe letting her return to Omaha until they were behind bars. Sitting at home waiting around for more intel felt brutal, but he knew in his gut that something was coming.

Kaylee nestled closer against him, as if sensing his unease, and her hand landed against his abdomen. Her touch soothed him, calming his frayed nerves. Her body was warm and welcome against his own, and after a long day of travel and time with his teammates, they were finally all alone in his quiet home.

"I liked waking up with you this morning," she admitted quietly.

He squeezed her thigh again, his thumb rubbing against the denim. "Me too. It kind of felt like no time had passed. Well, except we weren't sneaking around behind our parents' backs anymore."

She giggled and looked up at him, and when their eyes locked, it felt like something shifted in the air. Nick's hand crept slightly higher on her thigh. He heard her breath hitch, and his gaze slanted down. His big hand looked dominating and possessive on her inner thigh. Even though she was fully clothed, with a few quick movements, he could be unzipping those jeans and sliding his fingers between her silken folds. Giving her exactly what they both wanted.

Kaylee seemed to share his thoughts.

"Nick," she whispered, the air between them growing thicker. He didn't move a muscle, waiting. He'd give her anything, everything, but it had to be her choice.

Kaylee's cheeks were pink as she met his gaze, but when her lips parted, Nick couldn't resist her anymore. He ducked down and kissed her slowly, gently, his other hand landing on the back of her head as he held her where he wanted. She tasted sweet, like the iced tea she'd had with dinner earlier, and inexplicably like strawberries. His heart rate accelerated, and he sank his teeth into her lower lip, teasing her, before soothing away the sting with his tongue. Nick might want to pin her down on the sofa and completely devour her, kissing and caressing every inch of her skin, but he needed to draw this out. Go slow. Show her how much she'd always meant to him.

He took her mouth again, savoring the sweet taste of her, drinking down her sweet gasps and moans. This kiss wasn't a mad dash to the finish line like the night before. It was something softer. More tender.

This kiss felt like it meant something.

Nick ran his tongue over the seam of her lips, demanding entrance. Kaylee whimpered but opened to him, and then Nick was leaning her back on the sofa, his body carefully coming down over hers. She fisted his shirt, clinging to him, and Nick took his time as he stretched her out, enjoying the feel of her body beneath his. Her legs parted as he settled between her thighs, one wrapping around him. Even through their clothes, he could feel the heat of her core.

His erection was straining against his jeans, but he wasn't a hotheaded teenager anymore. This was about what she needed. What he could give her.

And Nick was about to drive her absolutely wild.

His tongue slid into her mouth again, teasing and tasting. Kaylee let him take control as she clung to him, and he wanted to roar in approval. She was so damn perfect for him, he almost hated to think of what he'd been missing out on all these years. Nick slid his tongue against Kaylee's, enjoying the eroticism of the moment. His dick was throbbing, and he lightly bucked against her sex, listening to her surprised little gasp.

Yes. He was hard and ready for her, but Nick was planning to take his time.

He tasted her again, thrusting his tongue in and out of her pretty mouth, and then kissed his way to her neck, smiling at her tiny little whimpers. Kaylee was so damn sensitive, and he'd always enjoyed exploring every part of her. He glanced down at his sweatshirt on her, male pride filling his chest. "I like you in my clothes."

"Funny. I thought you liked me naked best."

He chuckled, playfully nipping at her. "That too. I always loved you naked beneath me."

"Take me to your room," she said, her eyes wide with arousal. Kaylee's lips were swollen from his kisses, her cheeks flushed, and she looked so damn pretty it actually made his chest ache.

Nick raised his eyebrows. "You sure?" he asked, lowering his head to nibble on her neck again, making her squirm. "I'm happy to take my time exploring you here on the sofa."

In response, Kaylee wrapped her legs and arms around him, and he groaned as he felt the heat of her core rubbing against his straining erection. "I was planning to take things slow," Nick said, his voice strangled.

Kaylee shook her head. "I don't want slow."

Sliding one arm beneath her, Nick rose, his lips quirking at her squeal of surprise. He was so much bigger than her, he'd always been able to shift her around as he wanted. Her petite frame had always been appealing to him. Nick loved being able to take control as they made love and position her how he liked, then make her cry out in pure pleasure, coming apart on his cock or mouth.

He was moving toward his bedroom before he realized it, Kaylee secure in his arms. Nick set her on the carpet, his heart pounding. Her head only came up to his shoulders, and there was something so damn right about seeing her in his bedroom, in his personal space. Sure, he'd had exes, but it wasn't the same. It had never been serious, and Nick tended to stay over at their apartment. He stilled. Since moving into this home several years ago, he'd never had a woman in his bedroom.

Only Kaylee.

And he was about to take her to his bed.

She lifted her arms as he took off the sweatshirt. The green top she had on beneath clung to her breasts in an enticing way. Unable to stop himself, he palmed her full mounds, squeezing gently. "Nick," she pleaded, looking at his big hands on her body.

"I've got you, baby girl." Her top came off next, and then her lacy bra. Kaylee was breathing heavily, her breasts rising and falling. Nick wanted her completely naked before he laid her down in his bed. He knelt before her, kissing her flat stomach as she shivered. And then she was fumbling with her button and zipper, Nick brushing her hands away so he could slide the zipper down. Maybe it was caveman-ish, but he loved undressing Kaylee, baring her to his gaze. Her lips were parted again, her eyes heavily lidded, and he kissed the triangle of fabric covering her sex.

Nick could smell her sweet arousal, and as he pushed her jeans down over her hips, his fingers moved to her pussy, caressing her through her panties. He could feel her wetness as he touched her pussy lips through the material, and Kaylee whimpered.

"You're so wet for me," he said huskily, kissing her through the soft fabric.

Nick's arm wrapped around her, gripping one hip, and then he helped her step out of her jeans. As he looked up, his breath caught. Her breasts were full and creamy, swaying as she stepped free of the denim. The sight of them was mesmerizing. Intoxicating. They were rounded and full, with pert nipples, just begging for his touch.

Kaylee was a goddess. Creamy skin with a few stray freckles he wanted to explore. Sexy curves. Pink nipples and swollen, pink lips. She was toned and slender but had womanly curves he could get lost in. Gripping her hips, he kissed her stomach again. Teasing her, Nick nipped at the waistband of her panties. Her eyes widened in surprise, her lips parting, and then he was tugging them down with his teeth, easing his fingers under the elastic to speed the process up.

Nick reached over, yanking his bedspread back, and then helped Kaylee lie down on his bed, her naked form glorious before him. Her hair fanned out on his pillow, and he ducked down to kiss her, slow and deep. Nick quickly stripped down to his boxers, loving her eyes moving over him. She didn't cover herself or shy away, just let Nick's own gaze rake over her.

He was hovering over her again in an instant, kissing his way down her body as his erection strained against his boxers. He sucked on her nipples, leaving her wet and writhing beneath him. Nick growled as he licked and nipped the lower curve of her breasts, loving how she let him explore as he wanted. He cupped one full breast in his hand, his thumb skating over her nipple, and she bucked up on the bed, crying out.

Nick was dying to feast on her and abruptly rolled over on his back, instructing her to sit atop him. Kaylee hesitated only slightly before she straddled his chest, and then Nick was gripping her hips and lifting her over his face as she squealed in surprise.

"Nick," she gasped.

"Mine," he declared, her swollen sex mere inches from his mouth. He gave her no other warning before his mouth and tongue were on her. Nick ate her out, locking her to him with a firm grip. Kaylee whimpered and moaned, but he didn't let up, enjoying as she got wetter and wetter.

"Oh my God," she pleaded. "Please!"

He pulled her down impossibly closer, her legs spread wide, and licked and swiped at her arousal-drenched folds. Kaylee was shaking, her breath coming out in tiny pants, as he absolutely devoured her. Her hands gripped his headboard for support as she leaned forward, her heavy breasts swaying. She was so damn sexy it hurt, and he felt like he was going to explode right then and there as his cock swelled and balls tightened. Nick gripped her hips more firmly, then sank his tongue into her molten core. Kaylee cried out in surprise, and then she was riding him, seemingly unable to resist as he thrust his tongue in and out of her pussy.

It was sexy and erotic having Kaylee ride his

mouth. Although they'd made love countless times in the past, this was new for them. Nick realized he was probably more demanding in bed now that he was older, but Kaylee's eager responses told him everything he needed to know. This woman was made for him, for more reasons than he could say.

"My God," she moaned. "Nick. Oh my God!"

He eagerly tongued her, enjoying the feel and taste of her sweet arousal. Her thighs were trembling, her inner walls spasming around him. Nick slid one hand from her hip to her ass, cupping it firmly. His fingers teased the sensitive skin just below one cheek, caressing the tender flesh where her upper thigh met the curve of her bottom, and she gasped.

Kaylee was mindlessly moving her hips, taking what she needed, and he wanted to hear her explode. Nick shifted her slightly, his lips closing around her swollen clit, and with another swipe of his tongue, Kaylee screamed, coming apart for him. He continued lapping at her pussy, gently bringing her down, while keeping an iron grip on her body. She couldn't move if she wanted to, and he loved having her at his complete mercy, breathless and sated.

When she was trembling, he finally shifted her body back down, laying her atop him in bed. His mouth was coated with her juices, his cock rock-hard, but it was her head on his chest that made his heart stutter. His hands smoothed over her body, one landing on the small of her back, the other cupping her bare ass, enjoying the feel of her warm, soft skin beneath his fingertips. Words couldn't even describe the feelings coursing through him right now. Nick only knew that he'd do anything—everything—to keep her safe and make her completely his.

Chapter 12

Kaylee bit her lip as she watched the surveillance footage the following afternoon, her face scrunching up in concentration. West had hacked into the security system at her apartment complex and pulled the parking lot camera footage from a month ago, specifically the evening the two men had shown up on her doorstep. West was hoping to get a clear shot of them both and run facial recognition through their databases since she couldn't identify either man by name.

"Damn it. Those are grainy, too," Jett said as they watched the men looking around the parking lot, and Kaylee could sense his frustration.

"Can we enhance it?" Nick asked, his voice sharp.

"Maybe. Let's see what other angles we have of them," West said, clicking a few buttons on his laptop.

As Kaylee watched, she saw herself on the screen, her backpack slung over her shoulder. She looked terrified as she glanced around. The two men hurried her across the parking lot and helped her into a dark SUV. They shut the back door, and moments later, were driving off. West paused the video.

"Shit," Nick muttered, and she could feel him tensing beside her.

"That was sort of weird to watch," she admitted. "I wish they'd told me their real names, but that would make it too easy for them to be tracked." She shook her head, frustrated.

"They knew what they were doing," Nick said tightly.

"Look at the plate," West said. "That image is grainy, too, but we might be able to pull some of the letters and numbers. I'll have my guys work on it."

Jett's eyes were focused on the timestamp at the bottom of the screen. "Exactly twenty seventeen—8:17," he clarified, presumably for her benefit. "West was able to access some of the logs on base. You entered Offutt at eighteen-oh-four, just over two hours earlier."

"I wasn't there long," Kaylee admitted. "I heard the commotion in my office. We're in cubicles," she explained. "The higher-ups have office doors. I got my wallet and then got out of there. Cornwell tried to speak with me, but I ran. He wasn't about to chase me through the halls where other people could see us. I didn't even go to the grocery store like I'd planned, just headed back to my apartment. I must've gotten home around six forty-five. I was panicking and didn't know what to do. I almost called my supervisor, but again, I hoped it could wait until morning. Suddenly, those guys showed up on my doorstep."

"Cornwell came up with a plan on the fly and arranged for you to be taken into custody," Ford said, scrubbing a hand over his jaw. "He's probably worked with them before if he was able to arrange this so quickly."

"We'll figure out who they are," Nick said, his voice hard. He'd seemed angry as they watched the footage, and Kaylee knew exactly why. She was lucky she hadn't been hurt. Killed. Other women in her situation might not have been as fortunate.

"There's no footage from the time of the incident at your apartment yesterday," West said. "Whoever was involved in this was good. Or had resources. The surveillance cameras all stopped recording exactly fifteen minutes before the first calls to 911 came in."

"Damn it," Jett muttered.

"These guys could be anyone," Nick stressed. "Friends or subordinates of Cornwell. Hired guns. Military stationed elsewhere that received an order from him to move Kaylee to a secure location."

"Maybe they didn't know he was playing dirty," Ford mused.

"You think they're innocent?" Nick asked. "They had to realize they weren't actual Federal Agents." He'd shifted closer to her as West showed them the footage, his hard, lean body almost pressing against her own. She didn't hate it. As much as she'd become independent and self-sufficient over the years, something about Nick always made her want to seek shelter and safety in his arms. While she was safe here at their headquarters building, she appreciated his strength and support more than he knew.

"Let's review the news footage from yesterday," Jett said. "It's possible whoever did this stuck around to see the aftermath. I doubt we'll be lucky enough to catch those assholes on camera, but you never know."

West clicked on something on his computer screen, and the media stories from last night began to play on a TV at the front of the room. Kaylee felt sick watching the emergency vehicles at her building. What if someone had gotten hurt because of her? It was bad enough knowing her own things were ruined, but what had happened to her neighbors?

"We're going to comb through all of this," Jett said. "We'll also pull surveillance footage from earlier in the day. Maybe whoever was behind this scouted out the premises beforehand."

"Absolutely, boss," West said. "I'll make it happen." He lifted a phone on a secure line to make a call to his team, and Sam swore as more emergency vehicles raced to the scene on the television footage.

Sensing her unease, Nick guided her away. The other men watched them retreat for a moment before they got back to watching the video montage. They were conferring quietly as Nick moved her into the hallway, the space out there quiet. "You okay?" he asked, his brown eyes searching hers.

"Yeah. It's just a lot to deal with," she said, resisting the urge to shudder.

"And we've been looking over footage for hours. We'll take a break," he promised her. "If this gets us nowhere, we'll try another angle. West is hoping to get the plate from the vehicle they took you away in."

She looked up at him tearfully but nodded, and Nick moved even closer. "I hate seeing you cry."

"I'm okay," she assured him. "I'm just stressed out about all of it."

Nick had backed her against the wall in the hallway, his big body shielding her own. Even though anyone could come through the doors, it felt intimate standing there together. His tall frame hovered over her own as he made sure she was all right. While his broad shoulders and lean muscles always made her feel safe, the intense look in his eyes made her breath catch. Nick was former Special Forces, an absolutely lethal sniper, but when his focus and protectiveness was centered directly on her, she hardly knew what to make of it.

He lifted one hand and trailed the back of his knuckles over her cheek, and Kaylee felt warmth flood through her. The way Nick always treated her so carefully made her heart soar. He'd escorted her out of the conference room when he'd seen that she was upset. He'd held her so damn carefully in his arms last night. Kaylee suddenly felt overwhelmed by emotion. She'd thought she loved Nick when they were both teenagers, but he was the total package now. Smart. Strong. Funny. Protective. He was also insatiable when they were in bed The electricity between them sizzled even now in the office hallway, the heat from Nick's body warming her from within.

Her cheeks flamed as she recalled waking up naked in his arms this morning. She'd been embarrassed about the way he'd eaten her out last night, but he'd enthusiastically pleasured her again, tossing her legs over his shoulders and burying his head between her thighs. His tongue was both merciless and masterful, and Kaylee's cries of pleasure had quickly filled his home as he'd made her orgasm again and again.

Nick's eyes heated, knowing exactly what she was thinking, and he gave her a sexy grin.

"Nick."

"Kaylee," he countered, his voice thick with desire.

"Someone is going to come out here and see me turning bright red."

His lips quirked. "I didn't say a thing," he told her quietly. Nick ducked lower so that his lips were at her ear, his words for her alone. "But if you're wondering about whether or not I was thinking about this morning, with your pussy fluttering against my mouth as you came—"

"Shhh," she chastised, playfully swatting at him. She clutched onto his shirt though, not pushing him away. She'd been upset moments ago, and Nick had somehow managed to get her mind off everything that was going wrong. "Aren't your coworkers going to wonder why we're standing so close together in the hallway?"

"Nah. They all have women."

Now it was her turn to raise her eyebrows at him.

A look of amusement crossed over his face. "We're just talking in the hallway, Kaylee. It's fine. And while I hate that you're scared, I don't hate having you here in New York with me. I definitely don't hate having you in my home—or in my bed," he added, his voice low.

She licked her lips, staring at him. "We don't know how this is going to end, Nick," she said softly.

"I won't let anyone hurt you," he swore. "We're going to find out who those men are and make sure Cornwell is court martialed. And if you're worried about us? I want—"

Nick cut off abruptly as West stepped out into the hallway. Nick didn't move away, just glanced at his teammate. Kaylee's heart pounded as she wondered what Nick had been going to say. He wanted what?

"I think we finally got a clearer image of one of the men," West said, looking between the two of them. "My guys were running through the footage from earlier in the day yesterday, leading up to the fire. One person in particular was acting suspicious, and it looks like it could be a match to the guy in the grainy surveillance footage. Kaylee, could you take a look and confirm if it's one of the men who showed up at your apartment last month?"

"Of course," she said, her mind immediately snapping back to business as Nick took a step back.

Nick hovered behind her as they walked into the conference room once more, and then she sat down again, ready to look at images of the men who'd essentially uprooted her entire life.

Chapter 13

Nick's phone buzzed on the nightstand, and he muttered a curse, reaching over to grab it before the sound woke Kaylee. He'd been a light sleeper ever since joining the Army, which was both a blessing and a curse. He was always alert and at the ready and now had even more reason to be protective. While Kaylee said she hadn't slept well at the safehouse, she didn't seem to have trouble with him here, and a sense of satisfaction coursed through him at that thought. He loved that she felt safe enough to sleep in his arms every night. There'd never even been a discussion of him sleeping on the couch or Kaylee crashing in his guest room. He'd taken her to his bed the night before, and that was that. Now her few belongings were scattered about with his own things, and having her here felt so fucking right, he didn't want to ever let her go.

Fumbling with the phone, he blinked at the screen and saw a text from West.

West: We just ID'd the guys. Call me.

Nick: Got it. Give me a minute.

He sat up in the bed, scrubbing a hand over his eyes, and inadvertently tugging the sheets off Kaylee. She looked beautiful in the moonlight, her dark hair spread on the pillow, her creamy skin soft and enticing. The sight of her bare breasts made his libido rise. She had pretty pink nipples that he loved to suck on and tease. Kaylee had always been sensitive, and he enjoyed exploring various ways to make her come apart in his arms. Nick had held her against him earlier as he leaned against his headboard, one of his hands cupping her breast, the other between her spread legs as he fingered her slick folds. She'd been whimpering and begging for him in no time, and he'd brought her to orgasm, enjoying the sound of his name on her lips and her body arching against his, lost to the pleasure he was giving her.

They hadn't had sex yet, but Nick wasn't in a rush. They'd made love frequently as teenagers but somehow both knew that when it happened again, it would mean something. Kaylee was sexy and gorgeous, something to be treasured, and his protective instincts rose whenever she was near.

Readjusting the covers so she wouldn't get cold, his feet hit the floor, and he stood. Nick was wearing only boxers, but he grabbed his phone again and headed down the hall so as not to wake Kaylee. He stood in his kitchen, pushing the button to call West back, his body already tense and alert. West wouldn't call in the middle of the night unless it was urgent. The woman sleeping in Nick's bed meant everything to him, and he needed to know who these fuckers were that had shown up at her door.

"We just got ID on the two mofos who had Kaylee," West said, sounding surprisingly alert for the middle of the night. Vaguely, Nick wondered when the man slept. He seemed to always be on duty, helping out the team from the technical side of things.

"Who are they?" Nick asked, his voice harsh.

"Jarid Cronin and Kyle Levins. Both men are wanted criminals," West said. "How Cornwell became involved with them is anyone's guess, but they're both former military, dishonorably discharged three years ago. They're hired guns, taking under-the-table jobs, and they've evaded the law on multiple occasions to remain working underground."

"Hell. What are they wanted for?" Nick asked.

"They've got an entire laundry list of charges, the most recent highly concerning. They both have charges for abduction and rape. The last woman they held wasn't as fortunate as Kaylee," West said, his voice grim.

Nick's hands clenched into fists, rage coursing through him. He wanted to go beat the shit out of something, find these assholes and end them for even so much as looking at her. "Fuck," he ground out. "They're goddamn rapists?"

"She's lucky to have escaped unharmed," West said.

Nick saw red. He couldn't believe Kaylee had been kept with those assholes for a month. That an officer in the military had seemingly hired them, leaving Kaylee at their complete and utter mercy. "What the hell stopped them from harming Kaylee?" he asked, realizing his voice had risen. He glanced down the hallway, but didn't hear her stirring. His house was silent, and he focused back on his phone call.

"Money. They were no doubt given explicit instructions not to harm her. I believe Cornwell was biding his time. He needed a plan on how best to handle her, and he had no idea if she'd told anyone yet about what she'd witnessed. Kaylee ending up killed after her sudden disappearance would be suspicious given they were all in the same office that night. Records at Offutt would have each of them badging into the space."

"Motherfucker," Nick spat out, his voice quiet but deadly. "She could've been hurt because of him."

"They're not going to be happy that she disappeared," West warned. "If anything, Kaylee might be in even more danger now. Cornwell will still be looking for her, but now these assholes probably will be, too. They're not getting paid if she escaped from right beneath their noses. They're going to want her back."

Nick hadn't even considered that. He was in the situation so deeply, he felt like he couldn't even see things clearly. He was missing the big picture. "They can't track her here," he said boldly. "She took a bus west of Omaha to a small college town. They don't know who I am. Even if those fuckers were the ones on my tail leaving her apartment the other night, I had a rental car."

"We don't know the extent of their connection or resources," West said.

Nick huffed out a breath. "You think they got the plate and figured out who I am? Hacked into the records at the rental car place?"

"I'm saying nothing's off the table," West stressed.

"She'll be safe at my house," Nick said. "I'm not going to let her out of my sight. When I come in to headquarters, Kaylee will be with me then as well. Shit," he said, realization dawning on him. "You think these guys are the ones who offed the Security Information Officer?"

"That's a valid point. I'll see what I can find out. I wanted to let you know right away though. If they are looking for her, she'll be in trouble. Apparently, both were dishonorably discharged from the military because they were accused of assault. I hate to say it, but Kaylee was very lucky. Watch your six," West said. "It's doubtful they can track her to New York, but I can't guarantee they won't. She had her laptop with her. Her backpack. I think they would've already shown up if they had some sort of GPS tracker on her and were monitoring her movements, but I honestly don't know what to think about their capabilities."

"Roger that," Nick said. "I appreciate the call."

He set his phone down on the counter after West disconnected, looking around his dark kitchen. The only light was from the moon outside, peeking in through the blinds. His house was silent. Still. Suddenly, it felt all too vulnerable. He had locks on his doors and an alarm but not a security system like Jett did at his large home. He didn't have cameras around his property. If someone truly wanted to enter, Nick alone would be the one to stop them.

Uneasiness churned through his gut. For a man used to being on alert, lying in wait as a sniper, he was scared he'd miss something. Operating on foreign soil was different than monitoring things in Omaha or worrying someone might show up in his own backyard. He didn't think they had any way to track Kaylee after she'd left the safehouse, but what if he was wrong?

Chapter 14

Kaylee yawned and rolled over in bed several days later, loving the feel of Nick's hot, hard body pressed against her own. They'd spent every night together since he'd brought her to New York, and when she was in his embrace, snuggled up against him, it felt safe, like she was exactly where she belonged. Their days were spent at Shadow Security, trying to learn everything they could about Jarid Cronin and Kyle Levins. The two men had vanished after the break-in and fire at her apartment, completely disappearing without a trace. Cornwell had taken a leave of absence the next day, adding another wrench to the situation.

Through Jett's contacts at Offutt, they'd finally gotten an ID on the woman from HR—a twenty-something DOD employee named Fiona Brown. Nick was worried about the timing regarding Cornwell's absence, and so was she. It wasn't a coincidence that she'd snuck out of the safehouse, her apartment had been set on fire, and the man responsible for slipping classified intelligence to an unauthorized person was now conveniently out of the office due to a supposed emergency.

"We're biding our time," Jett had told her just yesterday. "We need to check all the boxes and have everything aligned before the authorities move in. Your job is secure," he assured her. "You'll be able to return to Omaha when this is over and not worry about your career being affected."

She bit her lip, her body tensing. Kaylee wanted to end this now, to have the military police bring Cornwell in, rounding up the other culprits while they were at it. She understood the need to wait until they'd gathered all the pertinent details, but now some of the suspects had vanished. No one knew where Cronin and Levins were, and that thought alone made Kaylee uneasy. If she went back now, would they be waiting for her to return?

She didn't think they'd be so careless with her a second time.

Jett had sent a man to her parents' home in Nebraska to keep watch. It was slightly alarming to realize how many resources Shadow Security had at their disposal. While she was thankful to have them on her side, she shuddered just thinking about anyone on the receiving end of their operations. This was Nick's life now, and she realized his work was probably just as dangerous as when he'd been in the Special Forces.

Nick began to stir slightly beside her, and she tried to relax against him once more. The quiet, early morning hours felt still and safe here in his bedroom.

It was hard to believe they'd reconnected only a week ago. Nick was gruffer than he'd been all those years ago, and way more intense, but he was still so damn gentle with her. It was almost scary the way her body responded to him. He was as attuned to her as always, knowing just how to make her come apart in his arms. Kaylee had tried to reciprocate, getting her hands or mouth on his cock, but he'd told her another time would be about him. They hadn't made love yet, and a part of her knew that when and if that happened, everything would change.

It would be hard to go back to Omaha when this was over. She stiffened. Kaylee didn't even have a place to go anymore. The smoke damage alone had ruined much of her furniture and personal belongings, according to the information they'd received from the local authorities. Sniffling, she felt Nick shift beside her. He was immediately awake, somehow sensing her distress, those dark eyes looking over her. "Hey. What's wrong?" he asked. One big hand reached up, swiping away a stray tear.

"I was thinking it will be hard to go back home after being with you for the past week, and then I remembered that I don't even have a home."

"You can stay here," he said gruffly, but his hands were gentle as he pulled her into his arms.

Kaylee pressed her face against his bare chest, feeling the masculine skin over his taut muscles. Tears fell down her cheeks, wetting his skin, and her body melted into his. Nick still had on his boxers, but she was completely naked. She didn't feel exposed or vulnerable though—just safe. Her breasts pillowed against his chest as he held her, her bare legs tangling with his own. She could feel his chest rising and falling, hear the sound of his heartbeat.

"Don't cry," he soothed, his voice low and husky. "I told you before that we'd figure this out, and I meant it. We'll get those traitors stealing intel, but we'll figure things out between us, too."

She huffed out a humorless laugh. "I work in Omaha, Nick. Even if being together like this feels right, we're still in two different places in life."

"So? Jett has graphic designers. We've got all kinds of people employed at headquarters. You've got a clearance now. You could work at Shadow Security and move in with me here in New York."

"Yeah right," she muttered.

"You could. What's stopping us?"

She sighed against him, not even having a response to that. It sounded simple when he put it that way. Although she'd been assured by Jett that she still had a job in Omaha, could she really return to Offutt? What had happened while she'd been in hiding for a month? What would she tell her colleagues about her sudden disappearance? People would talk whether she liked it or not.

Worry coursed through, and she sucked in a shaky breath.

Nick's hand trailed through her hair as he tried to comfort her. His touch felt reassuring, but deep down, she knew he couldn't solve all her problems. He'd protect her, yes, but what about everything else? She'd need to deal with her ruined apartment and her employer on her own.

"I know we just reconnected, Kaylee. I'm not an idiot. But we've stayed in touch all these years for a reason. If we've been given a second chance due to shitty circumstances, who am I to slam that door shut? Tell me this doesn't feel right."

"It's always felt right between us," she admitted.

"Damn straight. If you really didn't want to leave Omaha or your family, I could look for a job there."

She lifted her head, looking at him. "You'd just…give it all up? Leave behind your teammates and your home? The career you obviously love? You'd regret it," she told him forcefully.

"I'd regret letting you get away twice."

She closed her eyes in defeat, emotions washing over her. Nick was shifting them then, rolling her over. His lips brushed over her eyelids, her cheeks. Hot tears were spilling over, but he kissed each one away as he comforted her. "Don't cry," he murmured. His calm voice and gentle kisses soothed her, and she felt him trail his kisses to her neck. She tilted her head, giving him access, and one of his big hands cupped her breast, squeezing gently. His touch was more soothing than sexual, but she felt arousal stirring within her anyway.

Nick's erection was growing between them, straining against his boxers. Kaylee slid her hand down, cupping the length of it. She heard his sharp intake of breath. "Let me touch you, Nick," she pleaded.

He put his hand over her own, holding it still. "I'm going to explode right away if you do that. When I come, I want it to be when I'm buried deep inside you," he said, his voice thick with desire. "And when it's the right time? Nothing's going to stop me from making you mine."

He kissed her then, slow and deep, a promise without words as he pinned her wrists to the bed. She surrendered to him once more as Nick's hands and mouth soon trailed everywhere, making her lost to everything but him. When she cried out his name long minutes later, he kissed her fiercely, stealing her breath along with a tiny piece of her heart.

Chapter 15

Nick watched as Kaylee pulled open the bag of potato chips, dumping them into a large bowl. The skinny jeans she had on hugged her curves, but it was his oversized sweatshirt on her that made him smile. She'd ordered a few more things than what Lena had picked up for her but had taken to wearing his clothing as well. Nick loved the sight of his woman in his things. While they weren't officially a couple, she was in his bed every night, and he thrilled at having her warm and safe beside him. She'd thrown on one of his big tee shirts after they'd showered together this morning, and the sight of her bare legs and breasts pressing against the soft cotton had driven him wild. He hadn't been able to keep his hands off of her, and the eggs he'd been cooking had nearly burned.

She glanced over, flushing slightly as she realized he was watching her. "I like you in my clothes," he said.

"And nothing at all," she added with a wink.

His libido rocketed at that thought, but he moved around the kitchen beside her, bringing over several more bags of snacks. "Careful," he warned, ducking in for a searing kiss. "We have to get ready before everyone gets here." She licked her lips, her cheeks pinkening, and Nick locked eyes with her for a beat.

Kaylee in his kitchen was a temptation. Her sweet vanilla scent filled the air, and once again, he realized how damn lonely he'd been all these years. Clearing his throat, Nick grabbed the tomatoes, onions, and jalapeno peppers. He'd told her once she could stay, but he realized she didn't quite believe him. It wasn't a completely insane thought. They'd known one another for years, and when it was right, it was right.

"I can't believe you cook now," she teased as he began to chop the onion. "You're quite different than when we were in high school."

Nick shot her a sideways glance, a smile teasing his lips. "I can't believe you don't cook."

"Hey, I can microwave a frozen meal like you wouldn't believe."

He chuckled, expertly slicing the tomatoes next. "I bet you can. You were pretty good at microwaving popcorn back when we were teenagers. It's nice to learn that you've expanded your repertoire," he joked.

"Hey," she protested, tossing a potato chip at him.

Nick snatched it out of the air and smirked, stalking toward her. "Did you forget I'm a highly trained sniper? I can shoot a target from a thousand yards away."

"Oh yeah? You shoot potato chips?" she asked.

"Woman," he joked. "You wound me."

Kaylee pursed her lips together, smiling, and Nick moved in for another kiss. Damn. She was irresistible. At this rate, they'd be lucky to have things ready in time for dinner.

The rapping on the front door had them both jolting in surprise. "My teammates aren't supposed to be here for another hour," he said as he pulled back. Unease wound through him. He ducked to give Kaylee one last quick kiss then moved toward the front door, tension coiling within him.

Things had stalled in the investigation at Offutt. Cornwell hadn't merely taken a leave of absence—he'd vanished, along with Fiona from HR. It was believed they'd fled together as word of a classified intelligence leak stemming from the Air Force base had spread. Whoever was handling things at Offutt hadn't been good at keeping it under wraps. Maybe they hadn't wanted to. While it may damn well have been intentional on their part to let word of the leak spread, causing the guilty parties to be concerned, it burned him up to know everyone involved was seemingly in the wind. He wanted eyes on them to ensure Kaylee's safety. The last thing he needed was for any harm to come her way.

Nick looked through the window and was surprised to see Gray standing there. "What's up, man?" he asked, gesturing for him to come in. "I thought you couldn't make it tonight."

Gray nodded as Nick shut the door. "I can't stay but wanted to give you a head's up about what's coming. Kaylee here?" he asked.

"Like I'd let her out of my sight," Nick said,

shooting him a look of disbelief.

"I figured as much. I was on my way home and thought I'd stop by. Unfortunately, it involves her. I was leaving headquarters when I happened to see West."

"You were there on a Saturday?" Nick asked in surprise. While it was normal to work extra hours when they were readying for an op, that wasn't the case this weekend. While the tech staff had been busy on the case involving Kaylee, that wouldn't have included his teammate.

Gray lifted a shoulder. "I was working out. Plus, uh, Lena was handling some things there," he added in a low voice.

Nick snorted.

"I didn't want her to be there alone," Gray said. "Yes, security is around, but she doesn't like being in the basement of the building when it's nearly empty."

"Huh. I never would've figured that. She's always running errands for Jett, coming and going at random times," Nick said, his mind turning over that piece of information.

"Yeah, well, usually he's there when she is. It sounds like Anna wasn't feeling too well with her pregnancy, so Lena was helping out with the inventory. Jett needed to get things ready in case we're sent down to Mexico soon for the trafficking situation."

"And the gym is next to the armory," Nick said.

Gray pinned him with a look. "Don't mention any of this conversation to her. I don't want you giving Lena a hard time about it."

"Mention what?" Nick asked, clapping him on the shoulder. "I don't know her history, but yeah, I can see why a woman might not want to be down there alone in the armory on a weekend. Everyone's got a background check or security clearance at Shadow Security, but hell, you just never know the true side of people. Look at what's going on at Offutt. Cornwell is a highly decorated Colonel who's willingly passing on classified intelligence for money and sexual favors. He hired some fucking rapists to whisk Kaylee away."

"Exactly. Lena wasn't too happy that Jett needed this done ASAP, so I made sure that I was around when she was. That's all."

Gray's gaze shifted, and Nick glanced back to see Kaylee moving toward them. She looked cute as hell barefoot in her skinny jeans and white tank top. His sweatshirt was tied around her waist, her dark hair long and loose, and Nick felt something stir within him. She was gorgeous in anything she wore, but seeing her here, in his home, always made him want to roar in approval. Maybe that made him a goddamn caveman, but it felt like she was where she belonged.

"Kaylee," Gray said with a nod.

"You're early," she said, looking concerned as she came to stand beside Nick. "Is everything okay?"

"I was just at headquarters, and West told me about some photos he found," Gray said. "He'll be reaching out shortly, but I wanted to give you a head's up about them. It's not good."

"What sort of photos?" she asked with a frown.

Just then, Nick's phone buzzed, and he quickly swiped the screen.

West: I'm sending you some files. It's bullshit but will upset Kaylee.

West: Wanted you to hear it from me first.

Nick stilled, wondering what exactly West had to

show them. Kaylee looked up at him, the concern evident in her green eyes. "Did he find something?" she asked.

"I'm not sure," he murmured, waiting for West's files to come through.

"I haven't seen them yet either," Gray said. "It sounds like they're trying to use whatever it is in these photos against Kaylee."

Nick's phone buzzed again as a file came through from West. Moments later, his gut was churning, bile rising in the back of his throat. Even though he knew it wasn't real, the images before him made him sick.

Kaylee looked over before he could hide the screen and gasped in surprise. "Is that me?"

***

Kaylee felt like the world was spinning around her as she stared at the shocking slideshow of photos. Her heart raced as Nick quickly yanked his phone away. "Stop. Show me!" she demanded, tears smarting her eyes. It wasn't real. It was impossible. Her stomach lurched, despite her knowledge that none of it had really happened.

Gray had averted his eyes, giving them a moment, and Kaylee stared in horror at the fake photos that appeared to be her and Colonel Cornwell in various positions on her bed, both of them naked.

"But—but that's not me," she said, looking at the pictures in horror. "I've never slept with him. I barely know him. I've certainly never even invited him over to my place!"

Gray lifted his phone to his ear, putting it on speaker. "It's West," he told them.

"West, what the hell is this?" Nick asked, seething. He had an equal look of shock and horror on his face as Kaylee glanced at him, tears smarting her eyes. He couldn't think that these pictures were real, could he?

"These photos were blasted to the unclassified email addresses of people working at Offutt at approximately fourteen hundred this afternoon. Their IT staff blocked most of it, but several got through anyway. I'm trying to help them determine how the photos and email would've bypassed their spam filters and security. The photos weren't sent to any addresses on their secure network, as it came from an unclassified email address on an open server."

"I don't even know Colonel Cornwell," Kaylee told West. "I saw him at the office, but this isn't real. That's my bedroom, but none of this ever happened!" Tears filled her eyes as fear washed over her. Kaylee knew the photos were doctored, but would other people believe it? Her family? Her friends? An icy cold chill slid down her spine.

"It's AI," West confirmed. "Artificial intelligence. They took photos of your actual bedroom when they broke into your apartment, using it as the background. They generated AI models based on your physical descriptions. It was made to look exactly like you."

"But…why? Why would they do this?" she asked, frowning.

"Cornwell was mad," Nick surmised. "He wanted to implicate you in the stealing of classified materials as well. You witnessed it, and now he wants you to go down with him. Whoever broke in to your apartment only had minutes. They were probably searching for something, too, given the reports from authorities that they trashed the place."

"It's likely they were trying to find clues about where you'd gone," Gray said in a low voice. Kaylee's gaze flipped to him, and she saw a look of sympathy on his face. He might have a gruff personality, but she sensed he was just as protective as Nick toward those he cared about. She might not know Gray well, but she obviously meant something to Nick. Given that, Gray was as concerned as his teammate about her, and she felt herself softening slightly toward the intimidating man.

"That's absolutely wild that they'd come up with such an elaborate scheme," Kaylee said in disbelief. "They could've just planted classified materials there if they wanted me to look guilty."

"He probably didn't have them," Gray said. "If the HR woman photographed copies of the documents and sold them, Cornwell probably left the copies at Offutt to avoid being implicated if anything went wrong. It's a bad look to have stolen intelligence on you."

"Bad look," she muttered sarcastically.

"Looking bad is the least of his problems," Nick spat out.

"I know you probably don't want to, but look closer at the photos," West said over the speaker phone. "If you look at the details, you can tell it's AI generated."

"He's right," Kaylee said with a gasp. "Look how bad this is," she explained, peering at it closely. "I've got six fingers on that hand."

Gray's lips quirked. "Huh. It's almost amusing how bad it is when you look closely." Nick shot him a look that could kill. "But it's not funny that you were targeted this way," Gray continued, serious. "It's sextortion. It's not really you, but at a quick glance, people will think it is. Cornwell knew what he was doing. He wanted people to believe you were having an affair with him."

"That's sick!" she said.

"It won't hold up in court," West said in a clipped tone. "This 'evidence' of an affair between Kaylee and the Colonel is non-existent. There are multiple ways we can prove the photos aren't real and are simply AI-generated images. Some even look like they've been further manipulated with your actual face photoshopped on."

"It's still embarrassing as hell," Kaylee said with a shudder.

Nick was stiff beside her. Even though the photos weren't real, she could tell he hated seeing her in bed with another man. Nick muttered a curse as he hid the images on his phone. "How'd you find these?" he asked, his voice rough.

West cleared his throat. "Aside from the few that got through at Offutt, they were leaked online. We're running searches for mentions of Colonel Cornwell on the Web and got multiple hits. The photos and alleged affair are being played as a scandal—the woman scorned after her affair with a military officer ends decides to leak photos to embarrass him and sets fire to her own home to destroy any possible evidence."

"What?" Kaylee asked in disbelief.

"He was trying to shift the attention and focus to you. Stir up trouble. Cornwell has disappeared. Whoever is leaking this is making it seem like he's gone because of the scandal you're allegedly publicizing."

"He was stealing classified information!" Kaylee exclaimed.

Nick's arm wrapped around her shoulders, his touch soothing. "We know that," he assured her. "The authorities know that as well."

She let out a shaky breath, leaning into him for support. "Sure, you guys do, but what about everyone else? What about my friends and family? My coworkers? The people I work with will see this and think it's real! They'll think our alleged affair is the scandal."

"They'll think you were taken advantage of," Gray said. "They'll look at the photographs, just like we did, and realize all of it is fake."

Tears smarted her eyes, and she shook her head, turning and burying her face in Nick's chest. "It's okay," he soothed. "Cornwell will no doubt be court-martialed soon. The HR woman will be arrested. Before you know it, this will all be over."

"It's true," West said over the phone. "Our contacts at Offutt have indicated they have enough information to arrest them both. The incident you witnessed was far from the only time they'd met outside of regular business hours for nefarious purposes. The IT staff are already tracking the files Cornwell accessed before the occasions he met with Fiona Brown."

"They always met at work?" Nick asked, sounding surprised.

"Yes, that's correct," West confirmed. "They met right at Offutt on multiple occasions."

"The guy was only thinking with his dick," Gray muttered.

"I expect charges to be brought forth soon," West continued. "Conduct unbecoming of an officer. Unauthorized retention, removal, and transmission of classified documents. Likely more. They'll be located and brought in. Cornwell's estranged wife is being interviewed as we speak."

"What about the leaked intel?" Nick asked.

"The damage caused by the leaks is another issue. We probably won't know the extent of it for a while or any repercussions stemming from their treachery."

Kaylee kept her face pressed against Nick's chest for a few moments as the men continued talking, trying to compose herself. The people she worked with were supposed to have sworn an oath to their country. Not only were they traitors, they were horrible human beings. Her parents would see those fake photos. Her friends. Just because Cornwell might be arrested soon didn't mean the pictures would go away. And what harm had he caused by leaking Top Secret documents?

Sighing against Nick, she shut her eyes. They were murmuring about the men still missing as well, Jarid Cronin and Kyle Levins, and whether they remained a threat. Kaylee didn't think she could stomach this anymore. As the days continued to tick by, the entire situation seemed to keep getting worse, and she couldn't help but dread whatever might be coming next.

Chapter 16

Saturday night, Kaylee giggled as they sat around the dining room table at Jett's house, listening to Anna banter with her husband. Nick looked up at the sound, seemingly surprised to see her relaxed after the hellish week they'd had. The mercenaries Cornwell had hired were still in the wind, but Cornwell himself had been tracked to Florida with Fiona Brown. Cornwell had screwed up, using a credit card to check into a hotel in Miami. They'd both been brought back to Nebraska to face charges earlier that morning, and the team was celebrating the big break in the case over dinner.

"Really, Jett, just send me in next time," Anna joked. "I could've recorded Cornwell and his tiny dick and then blackmailed him. He'd never know what hit him."

"Like I'd let you anywhere near that asshole," Jett growled. "And I definitely don't want you looking at another man's package—no matter how little it might be," he joked as the table roared with laughter.

He leaned over and kissed his wife affectionately, Anna beaming, and Kaylee felt a strange twist of longing. It was obvious how much Nick's boss doted on his wife. Kaylee had been happy living alone all these years, but watching them, she felt like she'd been missing out on something.

Their nanny poked her head in the door, smiling. "The baby is down."

"Thank you so much!" Anna gushed. "You know it's rare we get a night alone together." She took the baby monitor from the other woman, setting it on the console behind the table. The entire scene felt so…domestic. And yet here Jett owned a multi-million-dollar security firm and ran a black ops team.

"So what exactly were Cornwell and his mistress doing in Miami?" Luke's girlfriend Wren asked from across the table. As an investigative reporter, she followed the news closely. This part of the story hadn't hit the mainstream media yet but no doubt would soon. While Kaylee knew that many of the team's operations involved classified things their wives and girlfriends would never know about, this case was national news. The entire country knew about the treachery of a military officer at Offutt Air Force Base.

"They were hoping to live a low-key life," Luke said with a shrug. "Although they planned to eventually flee to Mexico, Fiona had connections in Florida. Apparently, Cornwell went along with it."

"Jesus. Some men will do anything to get laid," Sam muttered.

His fiancée Ava elbowed him but clearly was trying

to stifle her laughter.

"He sold out his country because of his dick. He'll end up in jail because of it, too."

Nick smirked beside her, and Kaylee knew Sam wasn't entirely wrong. Cornwell had been cheating on his wife for years. He'd been baited this time, though, with Fiona Brown knowing she could trade sex for state secrets.

"Enough about work stuff," Anna declared. Her gaze landed on Kaylee, and a smile played about her lips. "We all know Nick's been pining away for you forever." Kaylee flushed as Nick muttered something under his breath. "Did you two really meet in high school?"

"We did," Kaylee said. "We were typical teenagers sneaking around behind our parents' backs. My mom always loved Nick though."

"What's not to love?" he quipped.

"I could name a few things," Sam started before Ava shushed him. "Just kidding, buddy," Sam said with a smirk.

"But you really kept in touch all this time?" Anna asked, her eyes beaming. "That's so romantic! First love," she said with a dreamy sigh. "Then there's Jett who picked me up at a bar in Manhattan one night," she said with a wink.

"She never left my side after that," Jett joked.

"Nick and I were both really young when we were together," Kaylee told the group. "When we reconnected, we realized we still have a surprising amount in common."

"And a lot hasn't changed. For instance, Kaylee still can't cook," Nick joked.

"Hey," she said, playfully swatting at him. He

caught her hand and brought it to his mouth for a sweet kiss, causing the women at the table to sigh and his friends to stifle their laughter. She knew she was flushing but couldn't find it in her to care. Barely two weeks had passed since Nick had flown to Nebraska. It felt like both a minute and lifetime ago. She could've continued on with her regular life, but to give up all this? She'd be missing out on a heck of a lot.

Kaylee cleared her throat. "It feels the same as when we were teenagers. That probably sounds cliché, but…." She shrugged. "We've always just clicked, you know? Our personalities are similar, and it's easy when we're together. We still share the same beliefs and have the same outlook on life. And Nick still loves watching reality TV shows with me," she teased.

"Huh. You sure about that?" Luke asked with a grin.

Wren smiled beside him. "I'm guessing he enjoys snuggling next to you on the sofa. He can hardly keep his hands to himself now," she teased.

Nick's arm was casually draped across the back of her chair, his hand on her shoulder, and his body was angled toward hers. "I'm not sorry about it," Nick said, his eyes glinting with amusement.

"Me either," Kaylee admitted, feeling somewhat shy.

He leaned over and pressed his lips to her temple, and she knew her face was flaming. His friends simply looked happy for them though.

"You work in Omaha," Sam said. "Are you going to steal Nick away from us when this is over? Drag him back to Nebraska?"

"I'm trying to convince her to move to New York," Nick said.

"'atta boy," Sam joked.

Kaylee bit her lip, suddenly nervous. Nick squeezed her shoulder, immediately attuned to her. "I don't know what'll happen," she admitted. "We'll have to figure things out. I'm afraid to go back with Cronin and Levins still on the loose. I don't have an apartment to go back to anyway."

The table grew silent, the ramifications of her words sinking in. She'd gotten settled at Nick's home, going shopping to get more of what she needed. Her days were spent at headquarters with him. She couldn't do any of the classified graphic design work she'd been involved with at Offutt, but she had been in touch with her boss. Her job was secure and would be there when she returned. If she returned.

"We're going to find them," Nick said, his voice harder than before. "Kaylee's not going to be living in fear forever."

"Damn straight she's not," Jett agreed. "Shadow Security doesn't take on jobs we don't finish. We'll track them down ourselves if the Feds can't do it."

"I don't want any of you to get in trouble," Kaylee said.

"We follow our own rules," Jett assured her. "You want strait-laced military rules and regulations? Fly out to California and see my brother."

The other men burst into laughter, used to Jett's bluntness. "His brother commands several SEAL teams in Coronado," Nick explained. "That reminds me," he continued, changing the subject. "I ran into Ace at Offutt when I flew to Nebraska."

"No shit?" Sam asked.

"Last person I expected to see there," Nick said with a chuckle.

"Who's Ace?" Kaylee asked.

"A SEAL team leader in Coronado. Good guy. We worked with him a couple of times when we were Deltas. Jett's brother Slate commands their SEAL team."

"Wow. An entire household of macho, military men. Can't imagine anything going wrong there. Thanksgiving dinners must be fun."

Jett smirked. "We're completely different, but Slate is a man you can depend on when the shit hits the fan. We balance each other out."

"Plus he loves me," Anna joked.

Nick's phone buzzed with a text, and he pulled it from his pocket with a frown. "What's wrong?" Kaylee asked, catching the expression on his face.

"Everyone's here. I can't imagine who'd be contacting me on a Saturday night."

Kaylee leaned over, watching as he pulled up his messages, an ominous feeling suddenly washing over her. The rest of the table had grown quiet.

West: Another photo of Kaylee has been released. It was posted online.

Kaylee's heart began to pound, and she watched as Nick thumbed a message back.

Nick: What's it a picture of?

She clutched onto Nick's arm, waiting for the reply. It had to be bad if West was reaching out to them now. The fake sex scandal photos had been bad enough. Fortunately, the AI pictures had been distorted enough that most people realized they weren't real. It was embarrassing as hell but hadn't brought as much negative attention as she'd feared.

Although the photos were online, most outlets weren't interested in sharing computer-generated, heavily-doctored images. She'd love to have them disappear forever, but that wasn't exactly how things worked on the Internet.

Kaylee still didn't know if Cornwell or the men he'd hired were behind it. Given that he was now behind bars, it seemed likely that Cronin and Levins were releasing the photos. What they hoped to gain from it, she wasn't sure. They couldn't exactly blackmail her when the photos were already shared publicly.

Nick's phone buzzed again.

West: Keep in mind it's likely not real. I haven't analyzed it yet.

Nick: What's in the damn photo?

West: It's a nude of Kaylee. Full frontal. They posted it online and threatened to send it to every single one of her email contacts.

Kaylee sucked in a breath, her stomach churning, and she felt bile rising in the back of her throat. "It can't be real," she whispered. "It's another AI trick, right? They have apps for that type of thing. It's sick, but they do exist."

"What'd he find?" Jett barked from across the table, grabbing his own phone.

"They have more photos of me," Kaylee said, her voice thin. Nick eyed her, seemingly knowing what she was thinking. "Tell him to send it. I want to see it."

Nick muttered a curse but shot off another text to West. A few seconds later, the image came through. Kaylee stared at the picture in horror. It was her in the bathroom at the safehouse, fresh out of the shower. Naked. Her breasts were clearly on display, a towel only partly obscuring her down below. The picture showed almost all of her completely nude.

She pushed back from the table, nearly knocking over her chair, and rushed down the hall to the bathroom, dry heaving. She could hear the commotion behind her, people asking if she was okay, and Nick's deep voice as he hurried after her.

She bent over again, emptying the contents of her stomach into a trashcan.

Nick was at her side in an instant, helping to hold her hair back as she heaved again. "It'll be okay," he assured her. "No one will really think it's you. They'll delete the photo if it's actually sent to them."

She gasped as tears streamed down her cheeks, and she shook her head, wiping her mouth with a few tissues. "It's from the safehouse. They must have been watching me the entire time. They had cameras somewhere in the bathroom. God. They probably have tons of photos. Videos." She burst into sobs as more tears streamed down her cheeks, and then Nick was collecting her in his arms.

His phone buzzed again, and he swore as he looked at the screen.

"What is it?" she asked, still clinging to him.

He was silent a beat, and Kaylee's stomach dropped. "Whoever posted the photo online just made a threat. They want you to return to Omaha, or they'll release everything."

"They won't let this go," she said. "Those men won't get paid for holding me at the safehouse with Cornwell now under arrest. Plus, I snuck out. There's no way he'd pay them anyway for not keeping better watch of me. They'll want money from me not to release more pictures."

Nick had stiffened, and his voice was hard as he met her gaze. "That's blackmail. Sextortion. You're not going to Omaha to meet with them. They will never hurt you, Kaylee. Never. I swear on my life I will hunt them down and make them wish they'd never been born."

She looked at him helplessly, her entire world suddenly off-kilter. "What can you do?" she asked tearfully. His large frame still hovered over her own, but she feared this was something even he couldn't fix.

Nick's voice was low but deadly when he responded. "I'm going to end them."

Chapter 17

Kaylee moved around Nick's bedroom the next morning, quietly getting dressed. She heard him already cooking breakfast in the kitchen, but he tended to wake up earlier than her to start the day. Too early, in her opinion, but she supposed it was thanks to his years of military service. He'd kiss her quietly and then get up, letting her catch up on another precious hour of sleep.

They'd left the dinner celebration shortly after the news of the leaked photo, and she'd slept fitfully. Kaylee had briefly spoken with her parents on a secure line from Jett's home, promising that she was okay and not to worry about any emails they may receive. A second photo had been posted, according to West, but she hadn't seen it. It was humiliating to know Jarid Cronin and Kyle Levins had been watching her the entire time she'd been with them in the safehouse. It was even worse knowing they were wanted men, charged with assault and rape. She knew how lucky she was that they hadn't harmed her.

Then again, they'd been promised a large sum of cash that had kept them at bay.

And now?

They'd be looking for her. She knew it. Although Cornwell hadn't been able to tie her to the leak of classified materials, the thugs he'd hired were ready to ruin her life unless she complied with their wishes. Everything about it made her feel sick.

Kaylee pulled a tee shirt on, grabbing a sweater to wear over it. She'd spoken with the investigators in Omaha yesterday and learned that some things from inside her apartment were salvageable. She'd need to go through her personal belongings and decide what to keep and what to toss. As the apartment itself needed to be repaired, her items would be packed and moved elsewhere. She hated all the different ways it felt like she'd been violated. If she hadn't forgotten her wallet, showing up at the office one Sunday evening, none of this would have ever happened. Of course, Cornwell would still be getting away with stealing classified documents. Lives could be at stake. She'd helped the greater good by accidentally catching him red-handed but at a cost to herself.

"Hey," Nick said as he walked into the bedroom. His gaze roamed over her, taking in the soft sweater and form-fitting denim jeans. "You look nice."

She smiled, but her heart wasn't really in it. Nick pulled her into his arms, and she relaxed into his warmth. "Gray will be over here soon to pick you up. Lena will meet you at the coffee shop. She's running some errands first."

"Are you sure it's safe for me to go?" Kaylee asked.

"Absolutely," Nick said. "While I hate letting you out of my sight, Gray will be with you the entire time. I think coffee with Lena will do you good. You've been stuck at headquarters every day with me dealing with this. You need a break. And trust me, you don't need to deal with these assholes any more than you have to. West is trying to track their location, but they masked their IP address. Still, he might be able to find out some helpful information from the metadata in the photos."

"It's weird, but they acted pretty normal around me," she said. "Some men leer and make women uncomfortable with their suggestive looks and comments. They weren't like that, at least not to my face," she said, frowning. "I guess they got their kicks from watching me in the bathroom." Fresh tears smarted her eyes, and Nick gave her a gentle hug.

"The investigator told me they found my cell phone in my apartment, so at least that's some good news. I've downloaded a lot of my apps on my new one, but I'd rather be able to use my old number eventually."

"We'll have West make sure there's no tracking software on the old phone before you get it back. What about your other stuff?" he asked. "Was there any word on that?"

"My clothing had a lot of smoke damage, but my insurance will pay to have it cleaned. We'll see. I've heard horror stories where the smoke scent would never come out of some people's things."

"You'll buy new things if you have to," Nick said. "I'm just glad you weren't there when it happened.

Did you want to use my credit card again to order some things here?"

"I'm okay for now. Thanks though."

His eyes were warm as he looked down at her. "I know you're more than capable of taking care of yourself, but I like taking care of you." His eyes heated as he looked at her, and Kaylee knew he was talking about more than just material things. There was a possessive look in his gaze that made her heart skip a beat. He was protecting her physically, guarding her himself or arranging for a teammate to be with her. He was sheltering her in his home. Cooking meals for her. And in bed? She flushed. He more than took care of all her needs there, too.

Nick brushed his lips against hers, teasing. "Let's go eat breakfast. We can't have you starving before you get to the coffee shop," he joked, taking her hand in his and guiding her down the hall.

"I'm going to miss this," she said, suddenly feeling sad.

Nick stiffened beside her. "Miss what?" he asked casually.

"When I have to eventually go back to Omaha."

Nick stopped, turning her in his arms, and backed her against the wall. She clutched onto both of his hands, loving the feel of their solid strength. His thick fingers twined with her own. "Don't go back," he said seriously. "I mean, sure, go visit and get your things sorted. But I was serious about wanting you to move here."

"It's so fast, Nick."

"Fast? I feel like I've known you my entire life. It just about killed me to let you go all those years ago. I always thought about you. Always. You're it for me."

Tears welled in her eyes. "But how can you say that after all this time? How can you know?"

He shifted even closer, pinning her hands to the wall, and she breathed in his musky scent, felt the heat from his body. "I know. I've always known. I left for you, baby girl. I couldn't do that to you then—make you wait around for my deployments, wondering where I was and if I was okay. You were still in high school when I enlisted. We were both damn teenagers then. It's different now that we're older."

"And you still feel the same way about me?"

He lowered his head, their breaths intermingling. Kaylee felt hot and cold at the same time. Being near him heated her blood, but the icy cold fear washing through her was real, too. Could she take that chance with him? Trust him with her heart? Could she admit to herself that she'd regret leaving him a second time?

"Why do you think I've kept in touch all these years?" Nick asked, his voice oozing over her like warm honey. "I feel the exact same way. You've always had my heart."

***

Coffee cups clinked together, and Kaylee heard the whirring of the expresso machine as she looked around the coffee shop. Gray had escorted her inside and was hovering behind her like the former Special Forces soldier he was. How Gray had gotten the job of babysitting duty, she wasn't exactly sure, but she assumed it had something to do with Lena.

Glancing over, she saw both Lena and Anna seated in a cozy booth, Anna's baby bundled up and sleeping in an infant car seat. Gray's hand landed on her lower back, and he nodded toward the other women as he guided her forward. "I'll stay here at the coffee shop but grab a different table. I know how you ladies love to talk," he joked.

"Thanks for bringing me," she told him.

"Of course."

While Anna waved flirtatiously at Gray, Kaylee noticed Lena and Gray exchange a meaningful look. While she couldn't begin to understand the dynamics of their relationship, she sensed it was more than either of them let on. Kaylee moved toward the women, smiling as she said hello, and Gray retreated to his own booth across the room.

"That sweater I picked out looks great on you," Lena said with a smile.

"Thank you again for doing all that shopping for me. Jett assured me he'd taken care of the bill, but I'm more than happy to pay you back as soon as I'm able to use my credit cards again."

"It's taken care of," Lena assured her warmly.

"I should've offered sooner, but let me know if you need anything," Anna said. "I'm going to be switching over to maternity clothes sooner rather than later with baby number two."

"What? You're hardly showing," Lena protested.

"My clothes are tight," Anna said with a laugh. She brushed her blonde hair back, her stack of bracelets jangling together. "That's reason enough for me. Oh!" she said, silencing the bracelets as her baby began to stir. "I really need to remember not to wear so much jewelry around him," she said.

"It's too loud?" Lena asked.

"That, and Brody likes grabbing shiny things,"

Anna said with a giggle.

Kaylee's gaze moved over the other woman. Anna was tall and slender, and as Lena had said, barely showing. Who was she to say what was comfortable for her though? Kaylee didn't know much about maternity clothes. As her eyes drifted over to baby Brody, for a split second, she imagined her and Nick with a baby. The thought was gone as quickly as it came, but as she turned the idea around in her mind, she didn't hate it. She could actually see a future with him, a family, just as he'd said.

Kaylee had more-or-less panicked earlier when he'd told her that she'd always had his heart. It had hurt to break up all those years ago, even though the decision was mutual and they'd both known it was right at the time. She'd grown up, gotten a degree, found a career she was proud of. And she could do graphic design work at Shadow Security just as easily as for the DEA, assuming Jett wanted to hire her of course.

Anna glanced back up at Kaylee after adjusting Brody's blanket.

"I think I'm set on clothes for now," Kaylee assured her. "Tell me what you ladies would like to drink. I'll go place the order."

The women each told her their drink order, and Kaylee moved to the line where the barista stood. She could feel Gray's eyes on her from across the room. He'd offered to get drinks when they'd first walked in, but she'd insisted she could handle it. While it was probably unnecessary to have Gray here, it did make her feel safer. No doubt Nick was busy at headquarters trying to find out where Cronin and Levins were hiding.

Kaylee walked up to the counter and ordered a vanilla latte for herself, then the two drinks for her friends. She swiped the screen on her new phone, checking her texts, then grabbed her wallet from her purse, accidentally bumping her phone into the card reader on the counter.

"Sixteen seventy-six," the cashier said, and Kaylee pulled out a twenty.

"Oh, it already went through," the cashier said. "You're good."

Kaylee looked at her in confusion just as a loud woman with two kids began ordering her own drinks from right behind Kaylee. Kaylee stepped out of the way, shoving her wallet back into her purse as their drink order was called. She glanced toward her friends, confused. Baby Brody began wailing just then, and Anna stood up and shushed him, hurrying past as she explained that she needed to change his diaper. Kaylee carried the drinks over to the table, noting that Gray was still watching them. Lena took her nonfat latte from Kaylee's hands, taking a sip, but her eyes slid to the silent former soldier as well.

"So, you and Gray?" Kaylee asked in curiosity, looking across the room to the gruff man. "He seems to be keeping a close eye on you."

"I trust him," Lena said lightly. "He might be a little rough around the edges, but we both have demons. He was hurt, too."

"Who hurt you?" Kaylee asked before realizing it wasn't any of her business.

Lena schooled her expression. "It doesn't matter. It was a long time ago."

Kaylee puzzled over that piece of information and took a sip of her own latte after she set her purse down. It wasn't overly sweet, just the perfect blend of coffee, milk, and flavoring. "Gray didn't buy these drinks for us, did he?" she asked, remembering what had happened at the counter.

"I don't think so. Why?"

"I pulled out a twenty to pay and—shit," Kaylee suddenly gasped. "My phone was unlocked. When I accidentally bumped it against the card reader, I must have used an app on my phone to pay for the drinks. My credit card is saved there," she said, worry coursing through her.

Lena paused mid-sip, looking concerned. "It's probably fine, but we better tell Gray."

Chapter 18

Nick moved authoritatively across the room at headquarters, listing to West call out coordinates to another member of the IT staff. The IP address used to post photos of Kaylee had been masked. Although West had been able to bypass their firewall, the person who leaked her photos had anticipated that, routing themselves through servers in countries around the world.

"They've got some serious skills," West said, typing something quickly on a laptop. "But they're not as good as they think. We're going to figure out where they were when they posted this." A map appeared on the screen, the various IP address coordinates popping up on the image.

"The threat posted online indicated that Kaylee should return to Omaha," Nick said. "I guess it's too much to hope that they're still there." He stood, looking over West's shoulder. The men had been hard at work all morning. While part of him hated being stuck here in New York, unable to move in, they needed specifics. Jett had warned Nick that the Feds would make an arrest when the men were located, but if they sat on this too long, Nick had no problem taking matters into his own hands.

West shook his head. "I don't think they were in Omaha when they uploaded this. None of these IP addresses are anywhere near Nebraska." He drummed his fingers on the table, multiple coordinates tracking by on his computer screen. Nick wasn't even sure what he was doing, but he was a sniper, not a tech guy. Finally, the program stopped, identifying one spot in particular. West grinned. "As of yesterday, they were in Miami, Florida."

"That's where Cornwell was arrested," Jett said, moving toward them. "They must have been down there because of him."

"They were trying to collect their damn money before he left the country," Nick guessed. "When Cornwell was arrested, they were forced to come up with an alternate plan—namely, uploading the images of Kaylee. While I'm sure they were using them for their own sick enjoyment prior to this, my guess is that they're now planning on blackmailing her."

"It damn well won't work," Jett ground out. "Not only will we have those photos taken down, but we'll hand their asses over to the authorities."

"After Cornwell was arrested in Miami, they probably left town. Maybe we can check the surveillance at the airports and get a location as to where they were headed," Nick said.

West nodded. "I can do that. Even if they were most likely traveling under aliases, we've got their photos now. I can scan the airport surveillance footage using facial recognition software. Again, while not entirely legal—"

"Do it," Jett ground out. "We don't know what else they're planning or what additional photographs they want to release. We also don't know if they ended up with any classified material themselves. When we get a location on them, we'll notify the authorities. Offutt is already fully aware of their involvement in this incident. They'll go through the appropriate channels and end this. I want to wrap this entire case up."

"Any word on how Cornwell and Fiona Brown are taking their arrest?" Ford asked, curious.

Jett muttered a curse. "She was questioned this morning and had a complete meltdown. She was crying, claiming that Cornwell forced himself on her. She said that he offered the classified documents as a form of payment."

"Bullshit," Nick spat out.

"No one believes it," Jett assured him. "She met with him on multiple occasions outside of office hours. They're tracking where the materials were sold, but she wasn't very careful with her newfound money. She's made several recent large purchases—diamonds and other jewels, a sports car, designer clothing."

"Damn," Sam said. "She thought no one would notice?"

"Maybe she wanted to be caught," West said. "Why else would they stop in Florida and not head straight to Mexico? She probably thought she could get away with blaming Cornwell for everything. It doesn't make sense to purchase all that if she was planning to permanently leave the country."

"She thought Cornwell would be arrested and not her," Sam mused.

"Either way it's fucked up," Nick said. "Dragging Kaylee into this mess isn't something I'll ever forgive or forget. I'm ready to end them."

"We will," Jett promised. "Cronin and Levins are dangerous men, but they're about to be brought to justice as well. Not a damn one of them are getting away with this."

Nick's eyes moved back to the laptop screen as he watched West work. They were so damn close to locating them, but he couldn't help but feel like something big was coming. It made no sense. It was almost like he instinctively knew that something would blow everything else out of the water. He'd relied on his gut frequently throughout the years. It had kept him out of trouble more than once, and he couldn't ignore it now. Everything in this particular situation seemed to be escalating: the fire at her apartment, the death of the security officer, Cornwell's arrest, the leaked photos.

They'd been here for hours but were finally making some good progress. Nick's phone buzzed, and he lifted it to his ear when he saw Gray's name on the screen.

"Everything go okay?"

"Yes and no," Gray said bluntly. "Kaylee is safe. She accidentally used an app on her phone to pay for coffee. Kaylee said it's linked to one of her credit cards."

Nick frowned. It was unlikely they'd track her via her cards, but not impossible. That's how the Feds had found Cornwell, wasn't it? He checked into a damn hotel with one. Uneasiness wound through him. "Appreciate the update. Watch your six."

"Will do."

Nick set his phone back down, the rest of the room continuing to work around him. He'd call Kaylee himself in a few minutes. Once he heard her voice, he'd be able to assure himself that she was okay.

Chapter 19

Kaylee walked out to the parking lot with Lena and Gray, zipping up her coat more tightly. She shivered in the cold air, once again noticing that Gray seemed practically immune to it. He was wearing a long sleeve tee shirt this time, which showed off his muscular frame, along with a pair of jeans. With his dark sunglasses on, he really did look like a bodyguard, alert and at the ready as he escorted them outside. Briefly, she wondered if he was armed. She knew Nick carried a weapon, so it stood to reason that Gray would as well.

"It's too bad Anna had to leave so early," Kaylee commented. "We barely got to chat at all. And she had her baby all bundled up in that carrier because it's so cold out today."

"Baby Brody was not about having the coffee date this morning," Lena agreed. "I think she thought it would be fun to bring him, but clearly he had other ideas."

"Gosh, I've always wanted kids, but babies seem like so much work," Kaylee mused. "Anna had the nanny helping her the other night but was a bit frazzled today trying to handle everything by herself. Anna didn't even grab her drink before she rushed out. Did she go right home?"

"I think so. That diaper change didn't go as planned, so she needed extra clothes for Brody."

"We should pick up something for her and drop it off. Their house isn't too far from here, right?" Kaylee asked. "I can grab her another decaf drink."

Gray seemed amused by her worry but agreed to drive her to Jett's home if she wanted to get something for Anna. He started to walk back toward the coffee shop with them, but Kaylee told him they'd be fine to quickly go in. He nodded but stood in front of the store anyway, his arms crossed as he watched them head to the doors.

"Is he always so intense?" Kaylee asked Lena.

"Always."

Kaylee giggled as they pulled open the door, still wondering what was going on with Lena and Gray. Lena wasn't ever fazed by him in the least. Even Kaylee had grown accustomed to his gruff mannerisms during the short time she'd known him.

The coffee shop was busy as they walked back in, but it felt warm and cozy compared to the artic blast outside. She moved to get in line, with Lena right beside her. "I'll pay this time," Lena said.

"Good idea," Kaylee said, worry suddenly churning through her again. She assumed Gray had texted Nick to let him know about the slipup earlier.

There wasn't much she could do about it now. She'd get Anna's drink and then be on her way. Kaylee placed the order and then decided to quickly duck into the ladies' room in the back as Lena swiped her own credit card.

"I'll come, too," Lena said. "Gray won't be happy if I let you out of my sight."

Shaking her head, Kaylee headed toward the back. "I'll be quick," she promised as they walked down the dim hallway. She felt oddly nervous all of a sudden. It was quieter back here, away from the hustle and bustle out front. A lone exit door was at the end of the hallway, and there was a separate area that seemed to house supplies. As she pushed open the bathroom door, she was relieved to see both stalls were empty. Not that she expected anyone to be waiting there for them, but for some reason, she was consumed with worry in a way she hadn't been earlier. Lena waited by the sink, and then a minute later, Kaylee was washing her hands.

"Her coffee must be ready by now. Let's grab it and head out," Kaylee said.

Kaylee's gaze fell on the changing table as they readied to leave the bathroom. Poor Anna. Maybe Kaylee should've offered to come back and help her earlier, not that she knew much about changing diapers.

"I'll text her to let her know you and Gray are on your way to drop something off," Lena said.

"Perfect, thanks," Kaylee said. "I wouldn't want to ring the doorbell if the baby is sleeping or something." She pulled open the door, walking into the hallway with Lena right behind her, then gasped as two men rounded the corner. Cronin and Levins stood in front of them, blocking the hallway. Kaylee and Lena were trapped, the back door at the very end of the hall the only way to escape. Kaylee opened her mouth to scream when they lunged, each man grabbing a woman.

One of the men covered Kaylee's mouth as he hefted her against him, his arms like iron around her. Kaylee kicked and fought, trying to get away, then sunk her teeth into his hand as he swore.

"Don't move a fucking muscle!" Levins seethed, pressing a knife against Lena's throat as he held her firmly in his grip. Kaylee froze, completely terrified as she stared at her friend.

Cronin set her on her feet, one hand still covering her mouth, the other wrapped around her upper arm, his grip like a vice.

"Go!" Lena mouthed to her. "Run!"

"One wrong move, and I'll kill her," Levins said, his face red, his eyes wide with rage. Both men seemed slightly crazed, like they were on drugs or some other type of stimulant. Within seconds, they were moving both women to the back door. Kaylee frantically looked around, unsure what to do. She might be able to break free of Cronin's grip, but she had no doubt Levins would kill Lena. The knife was still at her throat, and she had paled, her breath coming in shallow gasps.

Managing to slide her bracelet free, Kaylee let it fall to the ground as she was bodily moved out the back door. Gray was out front with no idea what was happening, but he wouldn't wait outside forever. He'd come looking for them. While he might not know the bracelet was Kaylee's, Nick would. And she didn't doubt that Gray would see it there. He was the type of man who noticed everything.

Kaylee's eyes smarted with tears as she and Lena were forced into the back ally and dark SUV waiting there. A third man was in the driver's seat, and as she was pushed down in the back of the vehicle, the doors slammed shut, and it raced away.

Chapter 20

Nick lifted his phone to his ear, concerned that Gray was calling again. West had been scanning the surveillance footage from Miami International Airport, running it through his computer system as they looked for Cronin and Levins. Nick was agitated. He hated knowing they were so damn close but still without a precise location for the two men. He wanted to end this. Immediately.

"Nick here," he said, stepping away from the laptop.

The rest of the team continued talking around him, monitoring the various feeds, but Nick was already moving toward the door, needing a moment of quiet. A third photo of Kaylee had been leaked that afternoon, with a note of warning. The men were demanding cash if she wanted them to hand over the photos. He'd have to tell her the bad news when he was home. Nick didn't want to let her know over a text message or phone call. She was already shaken up enough that they'd been watching and recording her in the safehouse.

"Kaylee's missing." Gray's blunt words bit into him, the complete shock to Nick's system scaring him like no enemy ever had before.

"What?" he asked, but he was already moving, rushing down the hall. Nick's heartbeat pounded his ears, adrenaline spiking through his blood. Nick nearly bumped into Jett in his haste, his eyes meeting those of his boss. "Kaylee's missing." He didn't stop and wait for a reply, just turned and jogged toward the lobby, phone still at his ear as Jett shouted out orders to the other men in the meeting room.

"Where did you last see her?" Nick demanded.

"At the coffee shop," Gray said, sounding anguished. "I escorted them outside, and Kaylee wanted to duck back in and grab a drink for Anna. Long story. Lena went back in with her. I was out front, waiting, and got distracted for a moment giving directions to a woman with a baby. When I turned back to look inside the coffee shop, they were gone. There was a to-go drink on the counter with Anna's name on it." He paused, and Nick felt his own heart thundering. "They never got it."

"Shit," Nick muttered, a sick feeling twisting through his insides. "Kaylee never would've left of her own free will. I'm on my way. See if you can find out anything before I get there. Question witnesses. Ask for camera footage. I'll try her cell." He pushed open the doors of Shadow Security, running to the parking lot. "What about Lena?" he asked.

It took Gray a moment to answer, and Nick could hear the agony in his voice.

"She's gone, too."

***

Kaylee cowered in the back of the SUV as it raced through the streets, taking turns more quickly than anyone would consider safe. She and Lena had both been pushed to the floor of the large vehicle, and Cronin and Levins were holding them down, seemingly eager for whatever was next. Lena was quietly crying, and Kaylee was too damn shocked and terrified to feel much of anything. These were men she'd trusted. She'd stayed with them for a month in the safehouse. They knew where she lived, knew where she worked. Yet the entire time she'd known them, they'd been watching her. Violating her privacy. Using her in ways she hadn't even realized.

Cronin grabbed some of her hair in his grip, yanking her head back so she was forced to look up at him. His muscular legs were on either side of her body, caging her in, and Kaylee had never been so terrified. She whimpered but didn't fight him, just trembled as she remained on the floor of the big vehicle. "I've waited a hell of a long time for this day. You've caused more trouble than you're worth," he spat out.

"Who are you?" she asked, her voice shaking.

"A friend of Cornwell, not that it matters to you. He owes us money, but I'm taking you as payment instead. You're about to become my own little fucktoy. I can't wait to get those damn clothes off you," he sneered. "My dick was hard the entire time we were in that goddamn safehouse. I jerked myself off every night watching you get undressed."

"No!" she cried out, unable to stop herself as horror washed over her.

He chuckled, tightening his grip. Her head was wrenched back uncomfortably, and she shook, hating the complete control he had over her. "I should have you suck me off right now for all my trouble. Why wait until we get to the house? Let me feed you my cock, princess."

"Enough!" the driver from the front seat roared. "Don't lose your goddamn head over this bitch."

Kaylee glanced askance at him, unable to move. She could only see the top of his head, a dark buzz cut, and broad shoulders. His voice was a low rumble of evil, and she had the distinct sense that he was even worse than the other two men. "You two idiots work for me, and you'll damn well listen to my orders. Cornwell might have fucked up, but we'll get our payday in other ways."

Cronin abruptly let go of her head, and she fell forward as the car turned again, awkwardly bumping against the front seat. Lena was silent and completely pale beside her. Kaylee had never seen her friend so terrified.

"How did you find me?" Kaylee asked, her voice weak. If she was going to be raped or killed by these men, she wanted to at least get some answers.

Levins smirked. "We had a hunch you were in New York. When Cornwell and his bitch were arrested yesterday, one of the Feds blabbed that Shadow Security was involved. The fucking idiot didn't even realize we were right there listening in. It was a nice piece of intel for us to overhear," he said.

"The timing was convenient," Cronin agreed. "With our source of cash under arrest, we still needed to collect our payment. Cornwell promised us one hundred thousand to hold you."

"I don't have that kind of money."

"Of course you don't, sweetheart. But we're taking you anyway. We'll have a little fun together. When we're through, the boss will sell you to the highest bidder. You'll never be a free woman again."

"No!" she shouted, anger bursting through her. If the men were surprised by her outburst, they didn't show it. "Rogers likes a fighter," he said with a grin, nodding toward the front. "We'll all take a turn with you. Maybe your pretty friend here can watch."

"No," Lena said.

"Don't worry. We'll give you a go, too," Levins said, licking his lips. "We only planned to nab the other bitch, but we can sell you both after we all have some fun."

The man driving glanced back at Lena, who cowered on the floor. Kaylee only got a view of his profile, but she didn't miss the look of lust on his face. "You won't touch her. That one is mine."

Levins chuckled as his gaze landed back on Kaylee. "No worries, boss. This one can take us both at the same time."

Kaylee gasped in horror, and Cronin laughed. "I'll admit we didn't know where specifically to find you," Cronin said casually, enjoying her discomfort. "We couldn't exactly stroll into Shadow Security, but we've been looking for you for weeks. Using your credit card was a bad idea. That led us straight to you, honey. We're going to have so much fun with you when we get to the house. Have you ever taken two men at once before?" he asked, his voice eager.

Kaylee began to struggle then, fighting to get up

off the floor of the SUV. The more she fought, the harder the men laughed. She wrenched around, trying to open the back door. They might be racing along the road, but she'd take her chances falling out of a moving vehicle. Anything was better than being held by these monsters.

As Kaylee twisted again, Cronin grabbed her hair, yanking her entire head back. "You're mine now," he seethed. "Don't move a fucking muscle."

Something pricked her neck, and then she slumped over, powerless, as darkness overtook her.

Chapter 21

"I've got a hit!" West barked out over the phone.

"Where?" Nick had raced to the coffee shop, arriving to find Gray, the police, and a crowd of onlookers already gathered out front. One woman was crying, saying she'd let the two men in the back door. Nick brushed past her, moving straight to his teammate, his phone gripped tightly in his hand as he spoke with West.

"Black SUV leaving the premises not more than thirty minutes ago," West said. "I got a plate from the cameras outside."

"Thank God," Nick breathed. "Can you track them?"

"Affirmative. I'll look through the traffic cams now to see which direction they headed. One of my guys is already trying to get the VIN number for the vehicle. I might be able to get a GPS off that and find out exactly where they're located now."

"Call me as soon as that happens." And then he and Gray were rushing to the back of the coffee shop, Gray rapidly telling him what had happened.

"This was on the ground," Gray said, showing him the bracelet as they stood near the back door.

Nick's stomach dropped. Kaylee had told him she hated not having any of her own jewelry or accessories, and he'd gotten the bracelet for her the other week. It wasn't anything fancy, just a simple gold bangle. She'd teared up anyway though, thanking him, and had worn it every day since. It had once again driven home how brave she'd been during the ordeal. Kaylee had left her apartment with barely any of her belongings. She'd been living in fear all this time, with the rest of her life put on hold. To get teary over such a simple gesture made him realize how much she'd been holding in and how much she'd been doing without.

When this was over, he'd go with her to Omaha and get things straightened out. Sort through her damaged belongings, help her purchase whatever she needed to replace. He hoped like hell she'd seriously consider moving to New York, but he'd do the long-distance thing for a while if that was what she needed. The fear inside him right now nearly slayed him, and it was all he could do to push those thoughts down and focus on finding his girl.

"I'm sorry," Gray told him as Nick looked around for any signs of a struggle. "I fucked up. I was literally right outside, and I knew she'd accidentally paid using the app on her phone. I knew she could be tracked. I never should've let her out of my sight."

"What's done is done. We'll find them," Nick promised.

The police were questioning witnesses around them, and Nick moved through the clusters of people, agitated. He wanted to push them all aside, comb every inch of the ground for more clues. He didn't have time to wait around for the police to question witnesses. Kaylee's life could be in danger. Nick stalked out the back door of the coffee shop, looking around. Sure enough, there was a security camera pointed right in his direction. Thank God that West had already hacked into it.

Jett and Sam pulled up into the back alley just then, both men jumping out so quickly, they left the doors open.

"Lena's with Kaylee?" Jett asked, the worry evident on his face.

"They were together," Gray confirmed. "They went back inside to get a coffee for Anna. Neither of them came back out the front door."

"We're going to find them," Jett assured both men, his face intense. "They haven't been gone too long, so time is on our side." He strode across the back ally toward the coffee shop like he owned the place, walking right up to one of the officers in charge.

"What do you need?" Sam asked.

"West is tracking the plate of the SUV they were in, but let's talk to the witnesses. Lots of people were around here. Maybe someone can give us further details until West can locate the vehicle."

"On it," Sam said, already striding away.

Nick's phone buzzed, and he lifted it to his ear. "Nick here."

"We're still trying to access the GPS coordinates from the SUV. From reviewing nearby traffic cameras, the SUV took off heading west. It followed the highway about two miles and then exited north on Shaw Blvd. We lost sight of it then."

"Got it," Nick said, making a circling motion with his hand to round up his teammates. "We'll head that way now." The men rushed over, and after Nick gave them the brief update, he climbed into Gray's pickup truck. Kaylee's vanilla scent slammed into him, and his gut churned. She'd been minutes from getting back into Gray's truck and heading home to safety.

"We'll find them," Gray said, his voice low and intense.

Sam and Jett were already peeling out of the parking lot, and then Gray gunned it, gravel spewing into the air as he raced away. "Hope the cops don't follow us," Nick muttered.

"I don't give a shit."

"Me either, but we don't want those assholes holding our women to know we're coming. We won't exactly be moving in stealthily if we've got sirens blaring behind us."

Gray didn't comment. Nick watched the shops and stores race by, Gray speeding up at yellow lights so they didn't have to sit at a red. He could see Sam and Jett up ahead. Gray's tires squealed as he took a right, finally turning onto Shaw Blvd. There were several industrial buildings here, but the road also led out of the busier area of town. The missing SUV could've headed anywhere—to a warehouse, a neighborhood off in the distance, a highway headed out of town.

Nick glanced down at his phone, almost expecting it to ring. "Where's West with the goddamn GPS?" he asked aloud.

"He's got our backs," Gray assured him, slowing down near the warehouses so they could scan the parking lots. Just then the coordinates from West came through. Nick called out the address to Gray, pulling up Google Maps on his phone to get directions. His phone buzzed with a text, and his hands shook as he read the message.

West: There's a third man with them. License and registration belong to a guy named Ivan Rogers. He heads a large North American sex-trafficking ring.

***

Nick jumped out of the truck fifteen minutes later, Jett and Sam already convening by their vehicles, weapons in hand. A large house surrounded by a perimeter fence loomed in the distance down the tree-lined road. "Fuck," Nick spat out as he walked closer. "We need eyes inside that home."

"Already on it," Jett said. "See that surveillance system outside? West said there are cameras throughout the interior as well."

"Can he get in?" Sam asked, his gaze swiveling back toward Jett.

"He's working on it. His team is trying to hack into the feed now."

Nick was staring at the large home, eyeing the massive glass windows on the front. If anyone stood looking out of them, he could easily get a clear shot. There were large trees in the side and backyard, but the front of the house was wide open. "I should've brought a better weapon," he said, his gaze narrowing. The sidearm he had holstered was nothing like a sniper's rifle. He could easily take a man out from here with the proper firepower.

"I'll have Luke bring additional weapons and gear," Jett said. He lifted his phone to his ear, speaking rapidly to someone on the other end of the line.

"We could get in there," Sam said. "Scale the fence, move in through the back and side yard. They'll see us coming, but if we approach from multiple angles, they likely can't stop all of us. There aren't many vehicles around. We could go right through the windows on the ground level."

"I don't like it," Gray said. "They could kill Lena and Kaylee before we're even inside."

"We need those camera feeds," Nick agreed, his pulse pounding. "I don't want to risk their lives breaching the home."

"But what if they're being hurt right now?" Sam questioned, and the men exchanged worried looks. He wasn't wrong. Kaylee and Lena could be assaulted while the team stood around waiting. They could be going through the worst moments of their lives at this very instant. Bile rose up in the back of Nick's throat. He took a step toward the house, and Jett's hand on his arm stopped him.

"They're on their way," he assured Nick.

A large SUV pulled up behind them, and Ford jumped out, rage crossing his features. "I was already on my way over to help. Luke is coming with additional firepower. Shit," he added, looking at the home in the distance. "That's a hell of a house."

"And the man who owns it is a hell of an evil fucker," Jett said. "West sent over a dossier on him. Ivan Rogers. Head of a notorious sex-trafficking ring. The Feds want him behind bars, but no charges have ever stuck. While he's not exactly flying under their radar, he's got other men doing his evil deeds and thinks he's untouchable."

"He knows Cornwell?" Nick asked.

Jett shook his head. "Cornwell knew Cronin and Levins from their military days. He hired them to keep Kaylee at the safehouse, but they mostly work for Ivan Rogers now. He owns multiple homes, both stateside and abroad. It was only the promise of a big payment from Cornwell that kept the men from assaulting her while she was under the same roof."

Nick saw red, his fists clenching Nothing would hold them back now. They would hurt her. Force her to do unspeakable things. He thought he was going to vomit simply thinking about what she was enduring.

The men all looked up in surprise as another car suddenly came speeding down the road. Within moments, Anna was stepping out of the vehicle, rushing toward her husband, the engine still running.

"What are you doing here?" Jett asked, sounding both alarmed and relieved that his wife was at his side.

"Lena texted me earlier," Anna said. She pulled her phone from her purse, showing Jett. Nick moved closer, and as he looked at the screen, stared at the messages in horror.

Lena: We're dropping off a coffee for you. Be there soon!

Anna: Sounds fab. xoxo

Anna: Did you get lost on the way over? No worries, but I have to feed Brody. Let yourself in.

Lena: 911

Lena: HELP US

"Why didn't you call me?" Jett asked, looking

astounded.

"I did! I got your voicemail when you didn't pick up. I had to leave a message," Anna said in a rush. "I tried to call you again on my way over, but my cell reception was bad."

"Shit," he muttered, swiping the screen on his phone to see the voicemail icon, then shaking his head. "That doesn't explain how you knew we were here."

"Lena gave me the login info to your 'find my phone' app months ago," Anna explained. "She said she had it because your whole life is on there, and you gave her access to track it in an emergency. She gave the info to me, too."

"Jesus," Jett muttered. "She's right, but I'd forgotten about that. She hasn't had to use it before."

"I raced over here as soon as the nanny came to watch Brody. Are they in that home?" Anna asked, looking toward the house in the distance.

"Yes. You could get hurt by being here," Jett said sternly, and Nick watched as tears filled Anna's eyes. "What were you thinking?"

"I know! Of course I know that, but they were in trouble because of me. They should've already been long gone, but they decided to bring me a coffee because I had to leave early." Tears slid down her cheeks, and then Jett was collecting her in his arms.

"You can't stay here," he murmured. "It's too dangerous. You're pregnant with our child, and I won't let anything happen to you. When Luke comes with the additional weapons, I'm having him take you home."

"My car—"

"I'll take care of it."

Anna pulled back slightly, looking from her husband to the home in the distance. "Are they okay?" she asked, her voice stricken.

"I don't know."

Anna looked over to Gray, and he muttered a curse. "I shouldn't have let them out of my sight. But the boss is right. You shouldn't be here."

"I'm sorry," she said, causing Jett to smirk.

"Of course, she apologizes to you and not her own husband," he grumbled. Anna didn't answer, just snuggled closer to him. Jett lifted his phone to his ear as someone from headquarters called, and it was all Nick could do to stand there and wait.

Fifteen long minutes later, Luke pulled up behind them. Nick rushed toward his vehicle, grabbing his gear from the trunk. Luke had brought Nick's rifle along with additional body armor, gear, and other weapons. Sam was already slipping on a bulletproof vest, readying to storm the house when it was time. "Thanks man," Nick said, sliding on his headset and slinging the rifle over his shoulder.

Luke met his gaze and nodded. They all realized the situation was growing more dire by the minute. West had finally hacked into the feed, but the women had been hustled upstairs, out of sight from the cameras. The surveillance system was on the main level, and unless someone appeared in the window, in Nick's sights, he couldn't exactly shoot through the walls hoping to hit them. Not when there were innocent women inside.

"We need a distraction," Ford said, scanning the area. "We need something to happen so they come to the window and look outside."

"Wouldn't they just check the security feed?" Gray

asked.

"Yes, so it's gotta be big. It can't be anything they'll go check on the monitors. It needs to shock the hell out of them so they rush straight to the windows. We need an explosion."

Chapter 22

"Where the hell are we going to get explosives now?" Sam asked with a frown.

"I've got a propane tank in the back of my SUV," Ford said. "I swapped out the one for my gas grill and didn't take the full tank out of my vehicle yet. Yes, I've been grilling all winter. Clara has pregnancy cravings for hamburgers," he said with a shrug.

"And thank God for Clara," Nick said, feeling a tiny twinge of hope. "If you position the tank out front, it'll pack a punch when it explodes and draw them to the windows. I'll lay in wait from here and can take them out. Just make sure it's far enough away so that the smoke doesn't obstruct my view."

"How many men are inside?" Ford asked.

"Three men were on the camera feed, along with Kaylee and Lena," Jett said, his voice grim. "West said two additional men were there earlier, but they left the location in a cargo van earlier."

"I'll take the propone tank to the edge of the

property, then shoot it from the woods across the street," Ford said. "When it explodes, you better believe they'll come running. Nick can lay in wait here, taking the kill shot when they appear in the window."

"And Gray, Sam, and I will prepare to move in," Jett said, taking his weapon from its holster. Luke had already driven away with Anna, and Nick could tell Jett was happy she was somewhere safe. He seemed more focused now with his wife gone. Nick didn't have the luxury of not worrying about his girl. Kaylee was inside, helpless. Within minutes, he hoped to have ended the entire situation with Kaylee safe in his arms.

The rest of the men grabbed their headsets and gear as Nick hustled across the tree-lined road and got into position.

"I've never heard of this Rogers guy," Sam commented as they jogged closer to the home. He'd left his mic open, and Nick could hear what the others were saying.

"His power has been growing in recent years," Jett admitted. "The Feds would love some charges to stick. He's smart."

"Not that smart," Nick countered as he clicked on his mic. "I'm about to end him."

"Take out whichever men appear in the window," Jett ordered. "We'll breach the premises and rescue the women. You'll have to hold back and provide cover. We don't know if anyone else will come running to help them."

"Roger that," Nick said. It killed him to lie in wait, but this was his specialty. His career. His life's work. The other men were trained in multiple weapons, but

Nick had been their sniper when they were on the Teams. Although he hated not being the one to rush in and get Kaylee, he trusted his teammates to get the job done. And he would end whoever stood in their way.

Nick watched as Ford came out of the wooded area, carrying the propane tank to the front gate. He'd be blocking access to the driveway when it exploded, which was smart as hell. If they tried to rush to their vehicles and escape, they wouldn't be able to go anywhere without going up in flames

Ford set the tank down and hastily jogged back to the woods. "I'm in position," he said over the comms unit.

"Roger that," Nick said, crouching down with his scope aimed at the windows on the front of the home.

Jett clicked on his mic. "We're spreading out around the perimeter. Everyone in position?"

"Roger."

"Roger that, boss."

Nick felt the slight breeze blowing past him and made minor adjustments to his calculations. He was counting on the men to appear in the big picture window on the second floor. Nick might only have seconds, and he wasn't about to miss the opportunity to take out the men who'd terrorized Kaylee.

"I'm ready at your word, boss," Ford said over the headsets.

"I'm in position," Nick said.

"All right. On my count," Jett ordered. "Three. Two. One. Fire!"

The crack of Ford's gunshot sounded almost simultaneous with the explosion. A loud bang reverberated through the area as the propone tank exploded, flames licking through the air. It was far enough away not to damage the house, and Nick still had a clear view of the second-story windows. It was also loud enough to draw anyone nearby closer to see what had happened.

"Come on, come on," he muttered.

Within seconds, two men appeared, looking out through the windows to the fire below. Nick took a shot, aiming at the first man's forehead. He shot the second man as the first was still falling to the ground. The shattering of glass could barely be heard over the secondary explosion. Something else had ignited near the propone tank, but the fire wasn't big enough yet to have reached the home.

"Two men down," Nick said calmly.

"Move in!" Jett yelled.

Nick watched a beat as two of his teammates scaled the fence, and then he was sprinting, moving toward Kaylee as fast as he could. Screams filled the air as he got closer, the women no doubt in shock, but nothing would stop him from getting his girl.

Chapter 23

Kaylee sank to the ground in terror, the explosion causing Cronin to shout a string of curses. To her absolute horror, when they'd brought Kaylee upstairs earlier, she'd realized that other women were being held in the home. Rather than immediately attack Kaylee, she'd been forced to watch Cronin terrorize his other victims, all tied up together in a bedroom. Part of her knew he hadn't raped her yet because she was heavily drugged. While he'd have no qualms about assaulting her, Cronin seemed to enjoy instilling fear in his prey. When she'd been unconscious, he wouldn't have had the sick pleasure of seeing her terror. She'd slowly come to, and he'd made her watch as he toyed with the other women, promising that she'd be next.

"What the fuck was that?" Levins roared, running past the open bedroom doorway. Kaylee watched him go, still slightly dazed, and then Cronin took off after him.

She scanned the faces of the girls and women being held in the bedroom, wondering where they'd taken Lena. Had Levins hurt her? Or that sinister man who'd been driving? She hadn't seen him since she'd woken up but knew he was probably here somewhere. The place felt like pure evil, and she jolted as the women began to cry and wail around her as they all heard a second smaller explosion.

A woman screamed as glass shattered in the large open landing upstairs.

Kaylee stilled, trying to organize her thoughts. Was that a gunshot? Another explosion inside the home? She fought at the ropes restraining her wrists.

Within minutes, the smoke detectors were sounding inside, no doubt from whatever was on fire in the yard. Cronin and Levins hadn't returned, and Kaylee feared they'd left her and the other women here to die. Tears streamed down her cheeks, and she froze as she heard male voices shouting. There was a thumping as heavy footsteps thundered up the stairs, and then Sam burst through the doorway, weapon drawn, dressed in full tactical gear. Several of the women started crying harder, but Sam was moving toward her.

"Are you hurt?" he asked, his voice urgent.

"No. I'm okay."

Sam pulled out a knife and cut her free from the ropes, updating his teammates over his comms unit. "I have Kaylee. She's unharmed. There are five other women in the room where she's being held. Nick, keep cover for us out front. I'm bringing them down."

Jett rushed into the room, his face tense as he barked orders into his microphone.

Kaylee almost fell over as Sam helped her to her feet, and he swore. Jett was beside her in an instant, his strong arm wrapping around her in support. "Gray has Lena. Let's get you out of here."

"But the women—"

"Sam's got them," he assured Kaylee, moving her out of the bedroom. She heard Sam talking to the other women in a soothing voice but knew they all had to be terrified. As they got to the stairs, Kaylee gasped in horror. "Don't look!" Jett ordered. It was too late. She'd already seen the bodies of Cronin and Levins, both with single gunshot wounds to the head. In the back of her mind, she wondered if Nick had shot them through the windows. She couldn't feel any remorse for the men who'd threatened to rape her and likely hurt those other victims.

"We're right behind you!" Gray yelled, carrying Lena in his arms. "She's unconscious. I think they drugged her."

"Is she okay?" Kaylee asked in fear as Jett hustled her down the stairs.

"She's breathing, just in a deep sleep. Let's move out!" Gray yelled.

In the next moment, Jett was hustling her outside. Nick was near the front porch, surveilling the area, the fire at the end of the driveway growing bigger. Kaylee could see their vehicles in the distance and hear sirens wailing. "I'll cover you!" Jett told him. "Come get your girl." And then as Jett lifted his weapon, readying for any danger, Nick was rushing toward her, pulling her into his arms.

"Nick," she cried, burying her face in his strong chest.

"I got you," he said, holding her tight. "Let's get

you out of here." She stumbled on the front steps, and then Nick was lifting her into his arms, carrying her to safety, away from the fire and chaos in that house of horrors. "There's a gate I found at the side. We'll go out that way. It's almost over, baby girl."

"You came for me," she said tearfully, looking up into his intense brown gaze.

"I'll always come for you," he swore.

A few tears did leak down her cheeks then, and Nick kissed her in the middle of everything, stealing her breath. "I love you," he said urgently. "I thought I lost you. You're it for me, Kaylee. I love you so much."

"I love you, too," she said, clinging to him tightly. "Take me home, Nick. I don't want to be anywhere else but with you."

Epilogue

One month later

Kaylee walked into Ford and Clara's house, smiling. Nick's arm was wrapped securely around her waist, his teammates and their women all gathered to celebrate. The living room had been decorated with both pink and blue streamers, balloons hanging in a fancy arch above the doorway, and gifts filled a table for the expectant couples.

"I can't believe you and Anna are having another boy," Sam said, clapping Jett on the back.

"They'll keep their mom on her toes," he said with a grin.

"I knew it was a boy," Anna declared. "It's early, but the baby has been kicking nonstop. He's going to be athletic and unable to sit still just like his daddy."

"Of course," Jett joked with a grin, but his hand landed on the back of Anna's neck, and he ducked down to brush a kiss against her temple.

Clara walked over to their group, rubbing the small

swell of her stomach. "And you're having another girl!" Kaylee said, feeling the contagious excitement filling the room. "Congratulations! That's so wonderful."

"Thank you. We're both so excited," Clara said.

Ford was right beside her, a huge grin on his face. "Guess I'm definitely a girl dad now," he quipped.

"They'll both have you wrapped around their finger," Nick joked with a chuckle. He squeezed Kaylee's hip, and she turned to him as the others moved away to talk with the rest of the guests. Nick leaned over, his mouth brushing against Kaylee's ear, a smile playing about his lips. "You've got me wrapped around your finger," he teased. "Just as long as you remember who's in charge in bed," he added huskily.

She blushed, and Nick chuckled and kissed the sensitive spot just behind her ear, making her heartbeat accelerate.

Kaylee had moved in with Nick several weeks ago, giving up her job in Omaha for a new career at Shadow Security. While their rekindled relationship had progressed quickly, it also felt right. She and Nick were truly together in every way. Nick was as bossy as ever in the bedroom, and his bold words reminded her of the way he'd bent her over their bed this morning after she'd showered. As his big hands had pushed up her silk robe, he'd run his hand over her smooth, bare bottom, his fingers sliding to her slick pussy. She'd been wet and aroused in no time, and then he'd sunk his throbbing cock deep inside her, filling Kaylee in the way only he could. As she'd looked to the side, her head pressed down on the bed, she'd seen both of their reflections in the bedroom mirror: Nick, virile and strong, his hard, lean body curling over her own; and Kaylee beneath him, flushed, her lips parted in a perfect O, her body his for the taking.

He'd thrust into her slow and deep until she'd finally cried out his name, her inner walls spasming around him. Nick had practically roared his own release, kissing her thoroughly afterwards while still buried deep inside her body. They'd made love every night since he'd rescued her, but this morning had been erotic, raw, and completely Earth-shattering.

"Maybe we can have a repeat tonight," he said huskily, seeming to know exactly what she was thinking.

"Yes please," she joked, and Nick's eyes heated.

"All right, we're almost ready to start!" Clara called out, looking around the crowded living room. "Thank you so much to everyone for coming. Ford says he doesn't mind grilling in the dead of winter, and I've been too tired to do much cooking lately. Hopefully a winter barbeque is okay with everyone to celebrate."

"It's perfect," Sam said with a grin. "I'm always ready to eat."

"We should've had Ford bring us donuts," Anna declared, winking at Clara. From what Kaylee understood, Ford had run out at lunch more than once to pick up treats for his pregnant wife and Anna.

"I'll put the burgers on in a few minutes. We can't have the pregnant ladies going hungry," Ford joked. He looked toward the table of food. "Where's the appetizer platter?" Ford asked. "I thought Lena was picking it up."

"I actually don't think she's here yet," Clara said, looking around at their group of friends.

"She left more than thirty minutes ago," Jett said. "Lena texted me to say she was on her way over."

Nick's phone buzzed just then, and as Kaylee saw him frowning, she glanced at the screen.

Unknown: I took back what's mine.

"What the hell?" Nick asked.

The rest of the team's phones began buzzing, too, the men grumbling as they received similar concerning texts.

"Has anyone talked to Lena?" Jett barked, and Kaylee looked around in alarm.

"I can't reach her," Anna said, looking slightly frazzled. "I just tried her cell and the office. There was no answer. Call her home number."

Jett was dialing it, muttering as the phone went to her voicemail.

Gray looked down at his own phone as it buzzed, his face ashen. "They took her!" Gray cried out, his voice anguished. "I just got a photo of Lena and a ransom note. That monster took Lena!"

"A ransom note?" Jett asked, storming over to Gray. He already had West on the phone, ordering him to track where the text messages were originating from. Anna started crying, but the rest of the room had momentarily gone stock still.

Kaylee gripped Nick's hand, terrified. "Is it him? That Ivan Rogers guy? Do you think he came back for Lena?"

Gray scrubbed a hand over his face, horrified, finally meeting Jett's gaze as he handed over his phone. Jett's jaw ticked as he stared at the photo, and the rest of the men began to spring into action, hurrying over. Gray cleared his throat, his voice hoarse with emotion. "She'll never survive being held captive again."

About the Author

USA Today Bestselling Author Makenna Jameison writes sizzling romantic suspense, including the addictive Alpha SEALs series.

Makenna loves the beach, strong coffee, red wine, and traveling. She lives in Washington DC with her husband and two daughters.

Visit www.makennajameison.com to discover your next great read.

Made in the USA
Columbia, SC
30 June 2025

60166657R00119